Gunfighter's Revenge

Center Point
Large Print

Also by James Clay and available from
Center Point Large Print:

Songbird of the West

**This Large Print Book carries the
Seal of Approval of N.A.V.H.**

Gunfighter's Revenge

JAMES CLAY

CENTER POINT LARGE PRINT
THORNDIKE, MAINE

This Center Point Large Print edition
is published in the year 2020 by arrangement with
the author.

The text of this Large Print edition is unabridged.
In other aspects, this book may vary
from the original edition.
Printed in the United States of America
on permanent paper.
Set in 16-point Times New Roman type.

ISBN: 978-1-64358-506-2

The Library of Congress has cataloged this record under
Library of Congress Control Number: 2019952042

Chapter One

Nobody paid much attention when Blake Crowley barged through the batwing doors of the Shooting Star Saloon. After all, Blake stopped by on most nights after closing down his gun shop. The perspiration that dampened Blake's receding hairline was not immediately apparent to the other patrons.

Blake headed directly to the bar. Stanley Wiggins, the barkeep, gave him a smile. "The usual?"

"There's nothin' usual about this night, Stanley. Wes Torveen is in town."

The smile vanished from the barkeep's face. "Who told you that?"

"Nobody, I jus' seen him!"

"Are you sure?!"

"Sure am. It's been seven years and he's grown a beard, but there's no mistakin' Wes Torveen."

The customary noise and activities continued at the Shooting Star. Men were gambling, buying drinks for the saloon girls, enjoying the artificial joy induced by alcohol. But at the bar, the situation was rapidly becoming grim as a group of men who knew Wes Torveen gathered. Their questions and remarks bounced about crazily like a child's rubber ball.

"Why's he in town?"

"We need to talk to his brother!"

"What good would that do? Owen Torveen can't control Wes no better than the rest of us!"

"Wes Torveen a gunfighter. Still seems hard to believe!"

"What's that the newspapers call him?"

"The One Arm Savage."

The chatter at the bar abruptly halted. Wes Torveen stepped through the batwings. The mood inside the saloon became more subdued as most patrons shifted their attention to the newcomer.

Torveen stood well over six feet. He was dressed in a black frock coat and a fancy gold colored vest. His entire wardrobe reeked of money, including the pearl handled six gun which was holstered against his left hip. His face registered a hard life, contrasting dramatically with the fine clothes. A beard the colour of night couldn't hide a large purple birth mark on his left cheek. Several scars remained as vestiges of assaults absorbed as a kid. His eyes were green, hard, and all encompassing, like those of a mountain lion.

Those eyes were now glaring at the men standing by the bar. "Well, well, ain't this a treat, some of my old friends from school days."

He walked slowly toward the bar. "Whiskey."

Wiggins's pudgy hands shook as he complied. "Sure, Wes, on the house, welcome home."

6

"My, my, so polite-like." He tossed down the drink and glanced at the bartender. "You're fatter than ever, Stanley."

The barkeep tried to look amused. "Guess so."

"Stanley, remember what yuh use ta say about my right arm, back when we was kids?"

"No, Wes, sure don't."

"You were quite the joker, Stan. Almost every day you'd say my arm swung back and forth like a pendulum on a clock. You'd ask me if I used the arm to keep time. Pretty funny, huh?"

Stanley shrugged his shoulders and looked toward the floor. "Yep, it's funny."

Wes Torveen banged the empty glass down on the bar and roared a loud, angry shout. "Then why ain't yuh laughin'?"

The entire saloon became quiet. Wes smiled broadly, revealing teeth heavily stained by tobacco. "Yep, I was born with a big purple stain on my face and a right arm that weren't no good. But I was right handed by nature. Couldn't use my left very well, so I was always droppin' things." He looked straight ahead at a medium sized man with stooped shoulders. "Yuh use ta get a lot of laughs from me, Ed."

Ed Horton spoke quickly, fumbling his words together. "We was jus' kids, Wes. You know how kids are."

Torveen walked slowly toward the part owner of the livery, as other patrons cleared away from the bar. "You're right, I know all about how kids are, Ed. They gang up on the weakest boy they can find. That was me. Yuh sure had yerself a good time knockin' me to the ground and spittin' on me."

The gunfighter was now standing inches from the hostler. Ed Horton could smell the mixture of tobacco and alcohol on Torveen's breath. "This right arm of mine is as useless as ever, Ed. Go ahead, have yourself some more fun."

"Wes, I'm sorry, I'm really——"

Torveen's left arm whipped upward in a barely perceptible blur. His fist shattered Ed Horton's nose. Horton slammed against the barroom floor and cupped his hands over his face.

Torveen's voice once again boomed. "I ain't spittin' on yuh, Ed. No man should ever spit on another man, treat him like he's not even a human bein'."

The gunfighter's eyes seemed to envelope every person in the saloon like an uncontrolled wildfire. "Josh Franklin, fancy seein' yuh again."

Franklin stood at the far end of the bar. He was even taller than Torveen. He had a well-tended red mustache. The owner of a large ranch he had inherited from his father, Franklin had bragged since childhood about his prowess with a gun.

"I recall the day my brother and I visited your ranch. You recollect it, Josh?"

Franklin was terrified but knew everyone in the

saloon was watching him. Years of bragging had caught up with him. If he didn't stand his ground now, he'd be laughed out of town.

"No, Wes, I don't recollect. You see I *own* that ranch now. Ain't got much time for thinkin' about school days."

Torveen experienced a surge of excitement. He was being challenged. The gunfighter had heard the quiver in the voice of Josh Franklin and saw the fear that ran through him like poison from a rattlesnake bite. This was going to be fun.

The gunfighter took a few steps toward his prey. "Well, Josh, allow me to refresh your memory. My brother Owen and me was real excited about bein' asked by Josh Franklin ta come visit him on the Franklin spread. We thought yuh were bein' right kind ta two boys from a hardscrabble ranch."

The rancher tried to back down without losing face. He leaned against the bar and attempted a casual laugh before speaking. "My momma made me go to Sunday school every week. Guess some of the golden rule took hold."

"Let me tell yuh 'bout how yuh handled the golden rule, Josh! Yuh got us ta ride up a hill out back of the ranch. Me and Owen had never ridden such fine horses. We dismounted and started playin' some game. The three of us got separated. Suddenly I saw yuh ridin' toward me with a pistol yuh must have hid in a saddle bag.

Yuh started shootin' at me, chasin' me all over the hill. One of those shots only missed by inches. Yuh probably would have killed me, but Owen rode off for your folks."

Franklin shrugged his shoulders. "Yep, guess I was a pretty mean kid. My pa took me to the shed good that night. Reckon I had it coming."

"I think yuh got a bit more comin' ta yuh." A deep, ominous growl crept into Torveen's voice. "What was that name yuh use ta call me, Josh?"

"Can't remember."

"I do. Yuh called me purple crip. Guess that's short for 'purple cripple.'"

Josh Franklin wanted to blurt out something about all that happening many years back. He was sorry: time to let bygones be bygones. But such talk would make him sound like the rest of the men in the bar: men who were afraid of Wes Torveen. He couldn't do that. Franklin took a step away from the bar. "Guess so."

"Well, Josh, I was born a cripple. Yuh became one on your own. Never earned nothin' in your whole life. As a kid, yuh lorded over ever one because your daddy was rich. Yuh had the ranch handed ta yuh when he died. Yuh think you're a big man, but that's 'cause you're crippled in the head."

A rush of anger overwhelmed Franklin's good sense. He went for his gun. The rancher

10

had barely touched iron when a bullet speared through his forehead.

A few of the saloon girls screamed and then a tense silence fell over the Shooting Star. The One Arm Savage had just shot down the richest, most powerful man in town. If he'd kill Josh Franklin, he'd kill anyone. No man who had bullied Wes Torveen was safe.

The silence was brief, broken by Sheriff Rob Laverty who ran through the batwings into the saloon. "What's going on here?"

Wes Torveen smiled benignly at the lawman as he holstered his gun. "A class reunion. Welcome Sheriff, good ta see yuh again."

Laverty's face went pale and a tremor ran through his body as he looked upon the horror that lay on the floor of the saloon. The corpse's face was masked in red, but it had to be Josh Franklin.

A finger poked at Rob's chest. "A fine man use ta wear that badge: Allen Hodge, heard he died 'bout eighteen months ago."

Rob Laverty was now staring directly into the eyes of the gunfighter. The anger he had displayed when he barged into the saloon was replaced by fear. He spoke through a dry mouth. "Allen was a fine man. Fine man."

Torveen continued to smile as he nodded his head in agreement. That didn't make the sheriff feel any better. "Yep, Robbie, I can remember a

11

few occasions when Sheriff Hodge stopped yuh and a bunch of other fellas from gangin' up on me. One time, he gave yuh boys quite a lecture. But yuh didn't listen none." Torveen's smile broadened. "Are yuh sorry you didn't pay more attention, Rob?"

A jumble of words came out of the sheriff's mouth.

The gunfighter cut him off. "I'm glad you're the law in these parts now. Yuh see, Sheriff Hodge would never cotton much ta what I plan on doin' in this town. He would stand against me, and I couldn't kill Allen Hodge, the only decent man in town. But I could kill you, Rob. Hey, what's a gunfight between two old school chums?"

Wes Torveen laughed as he began to saunter toward the saloon's doors. He suddenly stopped and rested his gaze upon the bartender. He pointed to the corpse, which was still oozing blood. "Better get that thing outta here, Stanley. Yuh never know when yuh might need the space for another body. Yep, that floor could get right crowded pretty soon. Good-evenin', gentlemen. I'm sure enjoyin' the class reunion."

Chapter Two

Reverend Thad Larkin stared out of his office window for a moment and then looked at the Bible which lay on his desk. He felt uneasy about the day ahead. In about three hours he would be presiding at the funeral of Josh Franklin. Franklin had been one of the wealthiest ranchers in Creekside, Arizona, but he had never made an appearance at the town's only church, at least not in the last six months since Reverend Larkin had become the pastor.

But Franklin's wife, Gloria, and their two young children showed up faithfully every Sunday morning at the Creekside Community Church. Gloria and the children were now staying in the hotel. Thad had brought them into Creekside himself two nights before when the sheriff almost shouted at him, "You need to git out to the Franklin spread, Preacher. Josh's been killed!"

The clergyman still felt confused by the whole ordeal. "What's the story on this Wes Torveen?" he asked himself in a whisper. "People keep talking about vengeance killings and——"

The church door banged open, shattering Larkin's private thoughts. Quick, desperate footsteps clattered toward his office. Someone was very anxious to see him.

Thad Larkin sprang from his desk, hastily opened the office door and saw Agatha Burke running down the middle aisle of the church. "I need your help, Preacher!"

Agatha was a thin, bony woman whose leather skin reflected a hard life lived on a small, modestly successful ranch. Reverend Larkin took several wide steps toward her. "What's the problem, Mrs. Burke?"

"Maddie, that fool niece of mine! She came into town with Dencel, the boys and me for the funeral. Now she's vanished. We can't find her nowheres. My husband and sons is out looking, but we need us more help!"

"I'll ring the bell!" The pastor bolted back to his office and retrieved the key to the church steeple. Thad Larkin was a man of more than medium height, in his late twenties. He had been an athlete in college and was a bit surprised when he had to slow his pace only slightly to accommodate Agatha Burke as they hurried out the front door of the small wooden building and ran around to the side. The door to the steeple was kept locked to prevent the bell from being rung by playful boys and drunken men.

"Don't worry, Mrs. Burke," Thad spoke as he entered the small enclosure and grabbed the bell's rope. "We'll find Maddie soon. There are a lot of good people in this town who will join the search."

Agatha looked uncertain. "Yes, and we got us some very bad men in this town."

Thad understood the point. Maddie Johnson was twenty and beautiful. But Maddie had problems no one could completely understand. The more polite citizens of Creekside called Maddie "slow." Others referred to her as "loco," "touched in the head," and there were even some who claimed she was possessed by a demon.

Everyone knew Maddie Johnson liked people and was far too trusting. And, yes, Agatha was right. There were some very bad men in town.

Reverend Larkin pulled hard on the rope.

Larkin left Creekside's one hardware store where the owner and several customers had expressed concern over the missing girl but had not been able to help. He paused on the boardwalk as he saw Owen Torveen hurrying toward him.

"No one at the livery has seen her today," Torveen said. "Rebecca is checking Sally's Dress Shop. Sis thinks Maddie may have gone there to look at the pretty dresses and hats."

Owen Torveen was one year older than his infamous brother and two years older than his sister, Rebecca. Like Wes, Owen stood over six feet, with a swarthy complexion. His face also reflected the many fights he had been in as a kid defending his brother. But Owen enjoyed normal health and didn't have to struggle with the disadvantages that plagued Wes.

"Let's check the Shooting Star," Thad replied. "Maybe somebody there has seen her."

As they did a fast walk toward the saloon, Thad continued to speak in a fast stream of words. "Agatha Burke is worried Maddie may be with your brother. She told me Wes and Maddie were close when they went to school together."

Owen nodded his head. "Wes is three years older than Maddie. Back in their school days that was quite a difference. But, yes, Maddie was friendly to my brother; guess it was because she's got problems of her own—"

Larkin cut him off. "Where's Wes now?"

"Don't know!" Owen replied as he pushed hard against the batwings of the Shooting Star and the two men rushed inside.

Thad's eyes quickly scanned the interior of the saloon. Something was wrong. The funeral of a prominent citizen had brought a lot of people into town creating an almost holiday atmosphere. But there were only a scattering of customers in the Shooting Star and they all had looked very sheepish when he and Owen stormed in.

"We're looking for Maddie Johnson!" Larkin shouted. "Has anyone seen her?"

The pastor's suspicions deepened. No one in the saloon looked at him. A few men placed a hand over their mouths, obviously covering smirks.

16

Thad turned from the customers and approached the bar. Owen was beside him. Hank Giles was standing behind the bar, busily wiping a mug that was already dry.

"How about you, Hank, have you seen Maddie?" the pastor asked.

"Ah . . . no," the bartender's eyes stayed fixed on the glass object. "What can I get you gents?"

"You can give us some information, Hank," Larkin shot back. "I think you're holding out on us."

Giles stooped down and slowly placed the mug on a shelf under the bar. "Don't know what you're talkin' 'bout, Preacher."

As Hank's head came up from behind the bar, Owen grabbed the barkeep by the collar and pressed his knuckles against Hank's wind-pipe. "Where's Maddie? We've already got us one funeral going on today, no reason we can't have ourselves two!"

Giles's face twitched several times, then he pointed toward a door to the right of the bar. Owen let go of the barkeep.

As Owen and Thad ran toward the door, Hank shouted after them, in a high pitched squeak. "Don't tell 'em I tole you nothin'!"

Thad flung the door open, revealing a short corridor and a back door that was already open. Behind the saloon was a forested area part of which had been cleared in the building of the

17

town. As Thad and Owen bolted out of the saloon they could hear the sound of men's laughter cutting a harsh blast through the trees and shrubs. A woman's voice, troubled and defiant, scorched through the merriment.

"That's Maddie!" The pastor said as he and Owen began to run down a path toward the manic noise. As they drew closer, voices became clearer.

"My, my, Maddie, so you're a real witch!"

"That's right, Mr. Crowley. But I'm a good witch. My special magic helps people."

"Well that's just fine, Maddie, 'cause I'm feelin' the need for some special magic right now!"

Lewd guffaws surrounded Maddie's scream. Thad and Owen pushed through thick shrubbery and into a small clearing as Maddie Johnson hit the ground. Blake Crowley stood over her. He was beginning to unbuckle his gunbelt. Crowley stopped, rebuckled, and gave the newcomers a threatening scowl.

"You jaspers can git back to where you came from."

The pastor helped Maddie Johnson onto her feet. As he did he realized the lady was in peril as were he and Owen. Blake Crowley's right hand now hovered over his Peacemaker. Blake not only sold guns, he had a reputation for being able to use them as needed. Blake had five accomplices, all of them wearing iron. One of those five men was Stanley Wiggins. Larkin didn't know the names of the other four, but he recognized the faces of the barflies.

Six men, all of them armed and all of them had obviously been drinking though it was barely mid-morning. It wouldn't take much to ignite a blood bath.

Larkin kept his voice a low monotone. "We're leaving, Blake, and Maddie is coming with us."

Blake Crowley was a man who enjoyed being the center of attention and he wasn't about to let this opportunity go by. "I'm disappointed in you, Reverent. It ain't right for a preacher to be spendin' time with a witch. Looks like that ol' devil has got a hold of your soul."

Laughter exploded from Crowley's friends. Encouraged, the gun shop owner continued. "Now a worthless sinner like me got him no problem with witches. In fact, me and my friends is kinda lookin' forward to spendin' some time with this . . . witch."

Another round of laughter was cut short by Maddie. "You better not say things like that, Mr. Crowley. I have powers. I'll use them. You'll see!"

Larkin was surprised by Maddie's use of the polite "Mr. Crowley." He wondered if the young woman had understood Crowley's intent when he pushed her down. Children frequently push each

19

other down in the school yard. Maybe she didn't understand . . .

Owen Torveen's voice stopped Larkin's speculations. "Maddie, don't talk about being a witch. You're no such thing!"

"Yes I am a witch! You better not say things like that, Owen Torveen! I'll cripple you. You won't be able to walk."

Torveen smiled kindly at the young woman. "Maddie, I want you to come away from here right now and stop spouting . . ."

Maddie Johnson closed her eyes and raised her right hand as if taking an oath. She began to hum or perhaps she was actually speaking words, Larkin couldn't tell which, and he was sure no one else there could. Maddie's eyes suddenly opened. Her right hand folded into the shape of a claw and she thrust it forward in the direction of Owen Torveen's left leg.

Madness seemed to flood into the young woman's eyes as she let loose with a cat-like hiss. Owen Torveen yelled in pain as he dropped to the ground. The rancher immediately tried to get up only to fall a second time.

"Maddie, please stop it, my leg hurts awful—"

"Do you apologize for saying I'm not a witch, Owen Torveen?"

"Maddie, don't—"

"Do you apologize?!"

"Yes, yes."

Maddie once again closed her eyes. This time, she remained silent as palm down she moved a hand across her body. When her eyes opened she returned the kind smile Owen had given her earlier. "Do you feel better now?"

Torveen brushed himself off as he returned to his feet. "Yes . . . ah . . . thank you."

During the entire drama between Owen and Maddie, Larkin had watched Blake Crowley, Stanley Wiggins and the other four men. They appeared to have at least half-believed Owen's theatrics. Maybe a new fear of Maddie's powers would end the confrontation.

As if to shatter Thad's hopes, Crowley drew his gun. "He's fakin'. Torveen is fakin' in order to scare us off."

"Don't be so sure," Wiggins cautioned. "There's stories about that gal which—"

"That's all they are, stories!" Crowley declared as his gun hand shook. He faced the young woman. "OK, Maddie Johnson, if you're so powerful, take this gun outta my hand. Go on!"

"I don't have to, Mr. Crowley. I've got a different plan."

"What might that be?"

"I'm going to make a man appear, a man who will help me," Maddie again held up a hand near her shoulder and closed her eyes. "He will come now!"

Confusion creased Blake Crowley's face, confusion which turned to fright as Wes Torveen pushed back a thick collection of branches and stepped into the clearing. "I see you're up ta old tricks, Blake. Pickin' on people who can't fight back; pointin' a gun at people who can't defend themselves. Yep, that's Blake Crowley for yuh, rawhidin' two gents who are unarmed 'cause they're goin' to a funeral."

Blake took two steps backward, his gun hand shaking even harder. "You're fast, Wes, but not fast enough to outdraw a man who already's got iron in his hand. I'm ending your plans for killing . . . right now!"

Wes's reply sounded casual and friendly. "Maybe so. But I was hearin' yuh talk 'bout Maddie's powers. Yuh know that girl really can work miracles. Why, she healed my right arm, it works jus' fine now."

Blake glanced quickly at his adversary's right arm. He didn't see the whip-like movement from Wes Torveen's left side. Crowley froze for a moment as he spotted the Colt now pointed at him. That moment cost him his life. Wes ignited a red-yellow flame into Crowley's chest. Blake Crowley stumbled backwards. He squeezed the trigger of his Peacemaker and singed the ground with a bullet. Wes's second shot sent Crowley into the dirt.

Several birds squawked as they flew into the

air, fleeing the violence below. Maddie Johnson began to cry.

Wes holstered his Colt and looked at Stanley Wiggins. "The Shootin' Star jus' lost a customer. Now, we'll find out if it's gonna lose a barkeep."

Wiggins raised his hands in a frantic stop gesture. "No, Wes, please no."

The One Arm Savage nodded at the four barflies who were now scattered about, all of them a safe distance from Wiggins. "I recognize those gents from last night. Yuh don't want 'em tellin' other customers at the Shootin' Star that Stanley Wiggins was scared of goin' up against a helpless cripple, especially a cripple who called him a fat hog."

Owen had an arm around Maddie, trying to comfort her. Larkin felt his words would sound hollow and meaningless to Wes Torveen, but he still needed to try. "One man has already died here Wes, that's enough!"

Wes ignored the pastor's plea. "What else do I hafta call yuh, Stanley, before yuh finally act like a man?"

Maddie broke away from Owen Torveen and ran to his brother. "Listen to Reverend Larkin, Wes. Please, he's right! I don't want you killing anymore."

The young woman placed a hand on the gunfighter's back and moved it up and down. Wes's body seemed to relax a bit and Thad wondered

23

if this small act of comfort went back to Wes Torveen's childhood when he was bullied and assaulted.

The One Arm Savage kept his eyes on Stanley Wiggins but his voice became soft as he spoke to Maddie. "So, it's *Reverend* Larkin is it?"

"Yes, Reverend Larkin is the best preacher in the whole world!"

Wes laughed softly. "OK, no more killin' today. Enjoy Josh's funeral, Stanley. You'll be joinin' him soon."

Wes turned and began to walk away. Suddenly, he stopped and faced Maddie. "You were a cute little girl when I left. You're a beautiful woman now, Maddie."

The woman blushed, looked down and covered her face.

"I'd sure like for yuh ta take a ride with me, if you're a mind. I'll get yuh back in plenty o' time for the funeral."

The young woman looked up. "I'd like that." Her eyes shifted to the pastor. "Reverend Larkin, will you tell Aunt Agatha what I'm doing. Tell her I'm safe and I will be back in time for Mr. Franklin's service."

"Maddie, perhaps . . ." Larkin started to step toward the young woman but was stopped by Owen's hand on his arm.

"It's all right, Pastor. Wes won't hurt her. They've been friends a long time."

Thad relaxed as Maddie and Wes made their way through the thickets. Larkin laughed softly before turning to Owen. "Strange thing, but I believe you. Maddie is perfectly safe with your brother."

Owen nodded his head. "I think Maddie understands Wes better than anyone. Me included."

Stanley Wiggins slowly began to leave the scene. He obviously wanted to remain a safe distance behind the One Arm Savage. The four barflies meandered behind him.

"I guess it's our duty to get Blake Crowley's body to the undertaker," Larkin said.

Owen looked in the direction of the corpse, and then looked back at his companion. "Yep, guess we should wrap him in something, and carry him out of here on a mule."

As the two men walked on the path they had run on only a short time before, Thad posed a question that had bothered him for some time. "I know Maddie . . . has problems . . . but how did all this talk get started about the girl being a witch?"

Owen's voice was solemn and low. "Don't know."

"You sure made good use of that superstition." Thad smiled. "That was quite an act you put on back there. Maddie must think she really has magic powers. And you took advantage of it. When you flopped to the ground, Crowley,

Wiggins and those barflies came close to believing it. You bought us some time."

Owen Torveen remained quiet. Not until they were once again behind the saloon did he speak. "You're giving me too much credit, Thad."

"I don't follow you."

"I wasn't acting back there. When Maddie made her hand a claw and pointed it at me, a horrible pain shot through my leg. I couldn't stand! I couldn't stand again until Maddie broke the spell."

Chapter Three

"I hope renting this carriage didn't cost you too much."

"Don't worry, Maddie; I've got plenty of money." Wes Torveen had intended his remark to sound flamboyant and joyous. It had come out sad and wistful.

"Besides, this ain't no time ta be ridin' horses. What with you wearin' that pretty dress."

Maddie looked at her hands and once again Wes felt his words had not been comforting. His companion's dress was old and faded.

"I don't really need a pretty dress. I only wear this on Sunday and at weddings and funerals. Weddings and funerals are sort of the same thing as church, don't you think?"

"Reckon." Controlling a horse from a carriage was different than doing it from the horse's back. Wes didn't have too much experience with carriages but he tried not to let it show. Making tasks look easy with one arm was a habit he had long ago acquired.

"I was sinning this morning," Maddie said.

"And jus' how were yuh doin' that?"

"I was going to Mrs. Mercer's store. She has a beautiful gingham dress in the window. I like to look at it when I can."

"How's that sinnin'?"

"Aunt Agatha says the devil makes me want stuff I can't have," Maddie replied. "She says that's coveting. I don't need a fancy dress."

"Besides, yuh never even made it ta the store this mornin', did yuh?"

"No, I was walking by the Shooting Star when Blake Crowley called to me to come inside. He said he wanted to talk to me about my powers."

"Maddie, never go inside a saloon, especially when a man calls—"

"I know, Aunt Agatha told me all about that. But I think she was talking about, you know, Saturday night. I didn't think much could go wrong on Friday morning."

"Men are what they are, Maddie. It don't make no never mind the time or day."

Wes brought the carriage to a stop. He got out and helped Maddie down. The girl could feel the muscular strength in her friend's left arm and shoulder. The couple walked hand in hand toward a nearby creek.

Maddie pointed to a large boulder. "Remember the crazy name you gave that big rock?"

"Nothin' crazy 'bout it," Wes protested jokingly. "I called it sitting dog boulder, 'cause that's what it's shaped like: wide and flat at the bottom, then comin' up and formin' a head. Well . . . sort of a head."

"This was our special place," Maddie smiled

28

and swung her companion's arm. "No one around to make fun of us. Remember the last time we came here? You were sixteen and I was thirteen. You told me you were leaving Creekside and you wanted to give me a good-bye present."

The couple stopped and faced the creek. Torveen picked up a small pebble and tossed it into the water. "Yep, I remember that day. I had ta leave this town in order to become someone else. I wasn't comin' back 'til I could settle some scores."

"You gave me a magic box. It's the best present I ever had."

"That box was important ta me. I was jus' startin' ta use my left arm really good. I made a small cross for my sister to wear around her neck, but that wasn't hard; the box was tougher. Makin' that box was sort of a turnin' point in my life. I wanted ta give it to a very special lady, a lady who was my friend when ever one else made fun of me."

"I wasn't a lady, I was just a little girl. And folks still make fun of me . . . most of the time. There are some who are nice because they need my magic."

Torveen picked up another pebble and this time threw it with more force. "What's all this jawin' goin' on in Creekside 'bout you bein' a witch? The magic box didn't cause all that did it?"

"The magic box is part of it, but I get my

powers from a certain place in the woods." As Maddie talked her eyes seemed to go out of focus. Wes recognized the look from when they were children.

"Maddie, yuh gotta stop all this crazy talk."

"It's not crazy. Oh, I make believe some of it. I saw you coming this morning before I told Mr. Crowley you would appear. But I really do help people and then they are nice to me. They're only nice to you, Wes, because they're scared you'll kill 'em!"

Torveen laughed quietly and rubbed his forehead. "Reckon."

"Don't do it anymore, Wes."

"Whatta yuh mean?"

"Don't shoot anyone else. I know you had to kill Mr. Crowley today, but it was just awful. Please, don't do it anymore. You're such a good person. You're not a killer."

Torveen stared at the water flowing past him. "Some people need killin'. They have it comin'."

"I know they were mean to you. They were mean to me too. Some still are!"

"Who are they, Maddie? Who are the people that treat yuh bad?"

"I'm not telling, because you'll hurt them. Reverend Larkin told me—"

"I don't go for that turnin' the cheek stuff!"

"I have an idea, Wes. Get all the cruel people

together in a room and have them say that they're sorry."

Torveen tried to suppress a guffaw but failed.

"Don't laugh! Having folks apologize is a lot better than shooting them. And Reverend Larkin is right. Sooner or later, hating people destroys the hater. He said that last Sunday. Don't let that happen to you!"

Torveen looked at the beautiful woman beside him and realized that inside she was still a child and always would be. But Maddie was a child in the very best sense: innocent, trusting and wanting to do what was right. The gunfighter realized he wanted this woman in his life . . . forever.

He drew Maddie close to him and kissed her. The move surprised the young woman but she didn't resist. She willingly moved her body into his. As they parted Maddie gently caressed the purple mark on his cheek. "You're the first man who ever kissed me."

"And you're the first woman I ever kissed without havin' ta pay for it."

Maddie was innocent but she had been raised in a town with two saloons and one brothel. The young woman knew what Wes meant. She laid her head against his chest. "I forgive you."

Those words amazed Wes Torveen. They implied an intimacy, a closeness and a possibility of redemption. The words should have sounded ridiculous but they didn't, not to Wes Torveen.

"Maddie, let's get married! Like I said, I got money. We'll go far away from here and start a ranch."

The woman took a step back and gave Wes a gleeful smile. "A horse ranch!"

Torveen's voice now burst with the joy he had tried to mimic earlier. "Sure, we can raise horses!"

"I'd love that. I could never raise cattle. Taking care of animals so they can be killed doesn't seem right. You raise horses to sell to folks who'll use them. That's the kind of ranch I want us to have!"

"Then a horse ranch it is!"

The couple hugged and indulged in several minutes of giddy laughter. Maddie's voice suddenly turned serious, though her face still reflected total happiness. "Will you stop killing people?"

Torveen paused and then nodded his head. "Yep, if that can keep yuh happy."

"And there's something I'll do to make you happy. I'm giving up my powers. Once we move from here I'll be away from these woods and, like I said, there is a spot in the woods where I get my powers."

Wes was uncomfortable with Maddie's talk about powers but decided to let it go by. "Say, do yuh think that sky pilot would be OK with marryin' us this Sunday afternoon? We'll leave town afterwards."

"I'm sure Reverend Larkin will. But let's not ask him until after the service on Sunday. I want this to be a real surprise. Aunt Agatha and Uncle Dencel and my two cousins go to church every Sunday, so they'll be there. They're the only ones I want to be with us at our wedding. Who do you want there?"

"Owen and my sis Rebecca. They go ta church too. They're family, but I'd bet they'll be happy to see me leave Creekside. Guess I can't blame 'em."

"We have to go back, now. I can't be late for Mr. Franklin's funeral."

"Sure." Wes took Maddie's hand and they began to walk back to the carriage. Exuberance still filled both of their faces. Wes gently kissed his fiancée on her forehead. "Can I see yuh after the service?"

"Oh, Wes, I wish we could, but no. You see, I have one more job to do as a witch. I want to do it tonight and get it all over with."

"Well . . . okay . . . sure." This time, Wes felt more than uncomfortable with Maddie's claims of being a witch. He couldn't ignore her talk any longer.

Chapter Four

The Burke Ranch was a ten-head operation which sold cattle to the larger ranches. Dencel Burke, Maddie's uncle, was a quiet, withdrawn man and his two twin sons seemed to take after him. Neither one of them had attended school as children, preferring to work on the ranch.

"Good thing them boys weren't in school," Wes Torveen whispered to himself. "They might o' beat me up and now they might be dead. That would sorta complicate matters with Maddie."

Torveen smiled inwardly as he watched the Burke's house. He knew his sudden proposal of marriage to Maddie had changed him forever and he was unable to get the joy of that change out of his system. The gunfighter had to fight down the giddiness that made him chortle at almost every thought. But he still felt a need to rout out the truth about Maddie Johnson being a witch. Maddie had never made such fool claims as a schoolkid. What had given her those crazy notions now?

The gunfighter had secretly followed the Burke family after the funeral of the man he had killed two nights before. Not surprisingly, the Burkes had headed directly home. Torveen was now hiding in a grove of trees where he had a clear view of the ranch house. Night came with a cascade of stars and a bright moon to make his spying an easy task.

Also making his task easy was Agatha Burke's booming voice. "So, how long are yuh gonna be at the Andersons?"

"Not too long," Maddie shouted back into the house as she stepped outside and closed the door.

The young woman patted her horse which was tethered to a hitching post immediately outside and then walked quickly to the barn which stood about thirty yards away. Before entering, Maddie looked behind her. She seemed to be checking to make sure no one was watching.

Maddie Johnson didn't stay inside the barn long. She quickly exited carrying what appeared to Wes to be an old potato sack. The girl returned to her horse, tied the sack to the saddle and was soon riding off.

Torveen knew where the Anderson farm was located. He trailed behind Maddie at a comfortable distance where he could hear the girl singing a hymn, *Blessed Assurance*. He hoped Maddie's singing was inspired, at least in part, by thoughts of their upcoming marriage.

Wes reflected on the fact that there had been very little love in Maddie's life. Owen had always been at his side when others tormented him. Maddie had to withstand cruel jokes and ugly remarks alone.

Dencel and Agatha Burke were decent enough folks, Torveen thought to himself. But they regarded Maddie as a burden and were impatient with her problems, maybe even a little scared. From what he could tell, the same could be said of her two male cousins. Maddie had a place to live, but after her parents had died when she was five, she never had a home.

"I'm changin' that," Wes said aloud.

There were no trees near the Andersons' small house. Torveen pulled up behind their barn, dismounted and tethered his horse to the ground with a pile of rocks. He glanced around the side of the barn in time to see Maddie entering the house.

Now the bright moon and stars were working against him. But a gunfighter must be fast in more ways than pulling a gun. Wes Torveen had often been the target of bushwhackers and had developed a sense of cunning and dexterity.

Holding his right arm with his left, Norveen folded into a jackknife position and ran toward the house. He stayed near a row of bushes which cast a modest shadow near the ground.

From those shadows he could see a curtain fluttering at the back of the house. He moved stealthily toward the open window and crouched under it. He immediately recognized Maddie's voice. "This is the last time I can help, so I'm going to try and do something really wonderful."

"You've helped us plenty, Maddie," came a gruff voice which Wes recognized as Gerald Anderson. The gunfighter recognized the next voice as coming from Gerald's wife, Alice. "We're embarrassed to be askin' again, but times are tough."

Torveen cautiously moved his eyes slightly above the sill of the window. Maddie and the Andersons were standing around a table. Gerald and Alice both had their backs to the window. Maddie was standing where she could see the window but did not notice him. Her eyes were fixed on the old potato sack which she had placed on the table.

Slowly the young woman pulled an object from the sack and held it in her hands. Wes's curiosity intensified as he recognized the magic box he had given her seven years ago.

Maddie opened the lid of the box. "I don't understand my magical powers, but I know I won't have them much longer. I want both of you to look inside the box like you did last time."

The couple complied with her request. "Nothin' there," Alice said. "Jus' like before."

"Magic, even good magic, works best in darkness," Maddie's voice began to take on a mystical, sing-song quality.

"Sure, anything you want," Gerald Anderson extinguished a kerosene lamp that was fastened to a wall. He then gestured toward a lantern which perched on the table.

"The lantern won't interfere." Maddie's eyes partially closed into slits. With one arm she clung the box to her as if holding an infant. She held one arm up and began a chant. Silence followed the chant, then Maddie opened the lid of the box and handed a large wad of bills to Gerald Anderson.

Both Gerald and his wife inhaled deeply as they counted the money. "Four hunnert dollars!" Gerald yelled. "That's twice what you got for us last time!"

Alice also yelled. "Enough to pay off the bank with some left over. Maddie, thank you so much!"

Maddie Johnson let out a deep breath and, still holding the magic box against her body, slapped a hand on the table top as if preventing a collapse. The table shook as the young woman began to breathe in heavy, erratic spurts.

Torveen's cautious instincts momentarily abandoned him. He shot up and almost cried out to the girl. If anyone had been looking at the back window, the gunfighter would have been easily spotted. But Maddie's eyes were focused downward and the Andersons were staring intently at her.

Wes hastily crouched down out of sight. He didn't try to peek over the window sill again but contented himself with listening to the voices.

"Can I git you some water, Maddie?"

"Thanks, but no, Mr. Anderson. I'm starting to feel better. Remember, something like this happened last time."

"Yep, remember."

There were more anxious questions from the Andersons and reassuring answers from Maddie. When it became apparent that the girl was getting ready to leave, Torveen scurried to the back of the barn where his horse was tethered.

He waited until Maddie rode off and then once again began to trail behind her. Maybe she would ride to that place in the woods where she claimed to get her magical powers from. That didn't happen. Maddie Johnson returned to the Burke ranch and took her horse into the barn, obviously to give the cayuse a rub down and food.

A restless feeling plagued Wes Torveen. He couldn't return to the home of his brother and sister, not yet. Without consciously deciding to do so, the gunfighter guided his horse to the creek where his life had changed about six hours back.

He dismounted and walked to the sitting dog boulder which he gave an affectionate pat. He then began to toss stones into the water. He didn't understand this witch business . . . didn't understand it all. But he knew it was coming to an end. Maddie was willing to surrender her magic for a life with him.

"Instead of followin' her around like she was a

crook, start countin' your blessin's, Torveen," the gunfighter spoke as water hurried by him.

Wes began to laugh as some ideas formulated in his mind. For the first time in his life he was experiencing happiness and he was going to share it, not step on it. Tomorrow would be a very happy day for a lot of people.

Still laughing, the gunfighter began to sing *Blessed Assurance*.

Chapter Five

Wes Torveen was sleeping soundly. His gun belt was slung over a bed post only a few feet away from his left arm.

Owen Torveen closed the bedroom door. His younger brother was down for the night, as was his sister. He could keep that appointment now. He headed for the stable and quickly saddled a roan. He was tense as he rode toward town.

Owen checked his timepiece after tying up his horse in front of the sheriff's office. It was a few minutes past three-thirty a.m. Following Josh Franklin's funeral, the lawman had whispered an order to Owen to "be in my office at three a.m. Don't tell nobody about this meeting. I mean nobody!"

As he entered the office, Owen received an immediate rebuke from the sheriff. "Took your time getting here!"

"I had to wait until Wes was in a deep sleep," Owen Torveen shot back. "I sort of got the impression you didn't want him to know about this friendly little get together."

Rob Laverty grimaced. His eyes did a quick scan of the ceiling. The sheriff was standing behind his desk, flanked by two men, both too restless to sit down: Stanley Wiggins and Ed Horton.

Laverty spoke as he built a cigarette. "Owen, your brother is out to kill all of us men who were in school with him. That is, all of us 'cept you. Wes trusts you. That's why you gotta help us."

"Just what are you getting at?"

"Tomorra is Saturday—"

"It's already Saturday, Rob, the day changes at midnight."

"Close your mouth, Ed!" Laverty put his tongue to the brown paper of the smoke and then continued speaking to Owen. "On Saturday you usually ride a buckboard into town to get supplies for the week. Do you think your brother will be riding along tomorra?"

"Probably."

"Make sure he does." Laverty swished a match across his desk and then put it to the cigarette. "Once the wagon stops in front of the Creekside General Store see to it that Wes stands up in the wagon for a spell."

"What for?"

The lawman fussed a bit more with the smoke before answering Owen's question. "I'm gonna be across the street from the general store, on the roof of the Rome Saloon. Stanley will be in the alley between the Rome and the saddle shop. Ed will be ready inside the saloon, which don't open 'til eleven. We're gonna ambush your little brother."

Owen looked around the room with scorn. "Aren't you gents brave!"

The sheriff pointed a finger at Owen. "Look here, Torveen! Your brother is a killer! Sooner or later, he's stopping a bullet. We're making it sooner," he swung his head in the directions of Stanley Wiggins and Ed Horton, "before he kills us."

"What we're doing is really self-defense," Stanley Wiggins's voice resounded with piousness.

Laverty waved his cigarette, sending red embers in Owen's direction. "Besides, the sheriff's office has always been helpful to you, Torveen. I'm sure you wanna repay the favor. So, are you with us or not?"

Thad Larkin was sleeping on a church pew. A couple of blankets made the hard wood a bit more comfortable. And by keeping all the windows in the church open, he could get a hint of coolness. For most of the year he slept on a cot in his office, but the office was a furnace in July and the cot too awkward to move.

He awoke to the sound of the front doors rattling. The pastor slid onto his feet, whisking the blankets to the floor. He did a quick stretch, and needed only a few long strides to reach the door. Larkin slept on the pew nearest the front doors of the church. The reverend was in sock feet. He slept with his clothes on. Late night disturbances were common.

Thad pulled the wooden bar from the door. He kept the doors barred during the night to keep out those drunks who used the church as a convenient place to sleep off a night of hoorawing.

A large man, stout but not fat stood on the church's doorstep. "Sorry to wake you, Thad."

Larkin glanced at the gray sky. "It's OK, I'd be getting up soon anyway, Fenton." The pastor's eyes shifted to the eight year old boy standing beside Doctor Fenton Stamford. "Hello Tommy."

"Hello, Preacher, we need to git ridin' quick."

The urgency in the boy's voice wiped the doziness out of Larkin's eyes. "I see you're wearing a gun, Fenton."

"You'll be needing one too," the doctor replied. "And like the boy said, be quick!"

Chapter Six

Ellen Brent closed the book, *Four Tragedies by Shakespeare.* "I shouldn't have tried reading this," she whispered. "My life has enough tragedy as it is."

She got up from the table and looked out the large living room window at the farm which would be hers for only two more days. What would Tom think of her selling it? They had put so much of themselves into building a farm, something they could be proud of, something that was theirs.

And then her strong, handsome husband got sick. Less than three months after first saying at the dinner table, "The food is fine, Precious, I just don't feel well," he died.

Ellen pressed her lips together. She wasn't going to cry. She had already done enough of that, and there was little Tommy to consider. She needed to be cheerful around the boy, assure him that the move to Denver would be fun and exciting.

Morning light was starting to push away night's darkness, but perhaps she should try going back to bed. There was still time for an hour or so of sleep. Suddenly an unfamiliar sound shattered her musings. Maybe one of the pigs was screeching . . .

A man appeared from behind the barn. He

walked stealthily along the side of the large structure and turned to examine the front doors. He didn't seem to be trying to get in. Besides, it was warm outside, no need to seek shelter.

"I'm a rich man! Can make any woman happy!"

This time, Ellen recognized the voice: Dean Ochs, a half crazy barfly who had tried to get fresh with her once when the family had ridden into town. Tom had warned him off and Ochs behaved himself from then on.

But Tom was gone now.

Dean Ochs was large and strong and pulled his gun at the slightest excuse. He sounded like he had been drinking but Ochs didn't really need alcohol to fuel his crazed behavior.

Ellen Brent froze for a moment, but only for a moment. She had to protect Tommy.

The woman exited out the back door and headed for the small corral behind the house where Tommy kept his buckskin. He was supposed to keep his saddle in the barn and Ellen gave a silent prayer of thanks that her son had disobeyed her and left the saddle on a pole of the corral.

She saddled the horse and hurried back into the house. Stones pierced her bare feet and Ellen remembered she was in her nightgown.

The woman entered Tommy's room cautiously. Ellen didn't want to alarm the boy but she needed to convey a sense of urgency.

"Tommy, wake up, honey."

"What time is it, Ma?"

"Tommy, I want you to ride into town and get Doctor Stamford."

"Are you sick, Ma?" Tommy's voice conveyed terror. He had already lost a father to disease.

"I'm OK, honey. But—"

A gunshot came from outside followed by a loud bellow. "I could buy this place if I wanna . . . make any woman feel like a queen . . ."

"That's Dean Ochs, the crazy man!" Tommy sprang out of the bed and began to dress; his thick blond hair flopping above his eyebrows. "Why's he here?"

"I . . . don't know. But I need you to get help. We're close to town—"

"Shouldn't I get the sheriff?"

"Rob Laverty is a fool." The anger in Ellen's voice surprised her as well as her son. "Doc Stamford will know what to do."

Tommy sat on the bed to put on his socks and shoes. "Some folks say the preacher is mighty good with a gun."

"Get Doctor Stamford, he's a good man, the mayor."

Ochs's voice again blared through the early morning. "I kin have any woman I want!"

Tommy's hands turned to fists as he stood up. "Let me stay, Ma. Pa taught me how to shoot. I can handle—"

"Tommy, do what I say!"

The boy's face went pale as he realized the extent of his mother's fear. Ellen embraced her son tightly. "I'm sorry to yell at you, honey, but you have to do what I ask. Your horse is saddled out back. Now, get moving."

Ellen followed her son as he made his way hastily to the back door. Tommy's face contorted as he turned and blurted out, "Don't worry, Ma. Bucky and I won't let you down."

This time the embrace was quick. "I know you won't!"

As the boy ran out the back door, Ellen realized she had to provide him with cover. Dean Ochs would hear him galloping off and her son could make an easy target.

The woman grabbed the Winchester which hung over the fireplace in the living room. She considered herself an average shot. She had brought down more than a few coyotes who had tried to attack their livestock. Then again, she had also missed more than a few . . .

No time for such thoughts. The woman glanced through the front window. Dean Ochs was now looking at the pigs fenced in beside the barn. He stepped back and yanked his six shooter from its holster. "Think maybe we'll fix us some bacon fer breakfast!"

Hoof beats sounded from the back of the house as Ellen stomped onto the front porch and fired the Winchester into the air. "Get out of here!"

The barfly turned and faced the woman. "Well, hello there, sweet thang. Glad to see you're ready to welcome an early morning caller."

Ellen levered the Winchester and pointed the rifle at the intruder. "You're not welcome here, Dean Ochs. Leave now or I'll shoot!"

"Ah, sweet thang, you're jus' too nice to shoot anybody."

Ellen's body trembled and every inch of her felt cold. Dean Ochs might be speaking the truth but she couldn't let him know it. "I've killed plenty of four legged coyotes. I wouldn't have any trouble killing a two legged one."

Ochs took a step toward her. "I jus' got somethin' to show yuh. Let me show yuh, then I'll leave."

"Stay where you are! Put away your gun and then you can show me."

"Sure, sweet thang." Ochs holstered his six shooter which made Ellen feel better but not by much. The barfly reached into his right pocket and brought out a wad of bills. "Know how much money I got me here?"

"No."

"One hunnert dollars. Betcha that man of yours never had a hunnert dollars in his pocket!"

"Don't you ever say a word about my husband, Dean Ochs, or I'll put a bullet right through your ugly mouth!"

The intensity in the woman's voice seemed to unnerve the barfly. "All right, all right, sweet thang, but you gotta think more like a widder woman. You need a man and I'm a man with a hunnert dollars and I can get me a lot more."

"You can get yourself on your horse and get out of here, Ochs."

"You're sure now? Not many rich men in these parts."

"I'm sure, leave!"

"OK, sweet thang. Left my sorrel behind the barn, hope we'll be meeting up in town soon."

Dean Ochs touched two fingers to his hat and bowed in a mock act of gallantry, then swaggered past the barn and out of sight. The sound of a horse galloping off filled the morning air. There was a trail immediately behind the barn. Dean Ochs could be riding off that way.

Could be . . .

Gripping the Winchester tightly, Ellen followed the intruder's steps. She moved cautiously past the side of the barn to the back. Yes, there were hoof prints in the dirt that lead to the trail.

Terror gripped the woman as she saw a sorrel down the trail, munching on the leaves of a tree. A blur streamed from a nearby cottonwood, grabbed her and knocked her over.

Ellen lay on the ground, struggling to keep her hold on the Winchester. Dean Ochs was on top of her, both of his hands on the rifle. He was laughing playfully.

"Yuh fell for an old trick, sweet thang. I jus'

slapped my horse and sent it off to make a little noise. Now, I'm gonna show you some more tricks."

Ochs was pulling the rifle toward him. Ellen's grip weakened. Her opponent was much stronger, the woman couldn't hold on to the weapon much longer. Ellen decided on a desperate ploy.

Employing all the strength she had left, Ellen pulled the rifle toward her. As she had hoped, Ochs used more force in an attempt to yank the weapon away. Ellen then pushed the rifle at her attacker's face. The Winchester smashed into Ochs's mouth.

The barfly fell sideways, keeping his hold on the rifle. With her opponent rolling in the dirt and moaning, Ellen ran for the front of the building.

Loud curses pricked the air as Ellen ran into the barn. The barn's double doors could be secured from the inside or out by a heavy wooden bar. The woman looked about frantically, where was that bar?

The curses grew louder. Dean Ochs was back on his feet and coming after her. She found the wooden bar, half covered by hay near the water trough, picked it up and made it back to the front doors as she heard the attacker's steps run to the house, then stop and come back to the barn.

The bar was now in place. Ochs pushed on the doors which barely moved.

"Open up, sweet thang. I'm through playing."

"Go away! My son's gone into town for help. They'll be here soon."

"Not soon enough, sweet thang. Better git you away from the doors."

Ellen took the warning as Ochs fired twice into one of the barn doors. He then used the butt of the rifle to pound against the weakened area, followed by a series of hard kicks.

Shards of wood sprayed inward. The continual blows made cannon-like explosions which resounded through the barn. The two horses that were stabled inside nervously whinnied and kicked at their stalls.

Ellen hurriedly climbed a ladder to the hay loft, then pulled the ladder up behind her. She buried herself under one of several piles of loose hay and listened as Dean Ochs forced his way through the cavity he had created in the door.

Making a small peek hole in the hay, Ellen watched her adversary stalk about the barn looking for her. His mouth was totally red with lines of blood beginning to cake on each side of his chin.

Ochs stopped and looked up at the hay loft. He laughed as he saw that the ladder was missing.

"Guess I found where you're hiding." He dropped the rifle and pulled his six gun. "Yuh haven't been nice to me, sweet thang, and I ain't feeling too kindly. Yuh come down, or I fill that hay loft with bullets and one of them is gonna find yuh."

A voice sounded from outside. "Throw down the gun, Ochs, right now!"

The voice was familiar, but Ellen couldn't place it. She saw Dean Ochs turn towards the barn doors.

"You're the sky pilot!"

"Never mind that, drop the gun and don't move."

"I ain't scared of no—"

Ellen watched as Dean Ochs shifted his gun hand, obviously getting ready to fire. He never got the chance. A shot sounded and Ochs staggered backwards; he tried to raise his gun but couldn't. He dropped to the floor.

Stunned, Ellen remained where she was as Thad Larkin came running in. When the woman recognized Reverend Larkin she was stunned a second time: not often do you see a preacher carrying a Colt .45. Her son's shouts cut short those thoughts.

"Ma, where are you, are you all right?"

Ellen Beck stood up and waved. "I'm fine, Tommy, and proud of my son!"

Fenton Stamford's bulk slowed down his progress through the hole in the door but he soon joined Tommy in taking the ladder from Ellen and steadying it as she climbed down. The barn filled with Tommy's excited shouts.

Larkin crouched over the man he had just shot. The pastor recognized Dean Ochs as one of the barflies who had accompanied Blake Crowley the day before in what was an attempt to gang rape Maddie. Tommy had told him the intruder's name as they rode to the farm.

The dying man looked at the pastor scornfully. "Don't be proud of what yuh done, Preacher. It weren't you . . . was Maddie."

"What do you mean?"

"She did good for me . . . gave me magic money. Then, I tried . . . yesterday . . . yuh know . . . musta made her mad, she put a curse on me . . . curse . . ."

Dean Ochs babbled a few more words but Thad couldn't make them out. He tried to ask a question about the magic money but Ochs didn't respond. When the pastor felt for a pulse on the man's neck he knew why.

Ellen Brent was hugging Tommy as both of them indulged in the laughter that comes when pent up emotions are unleashed. Doctor Stamford stood by making jokes.

"We have our pastor right here. We'll give that drunk's magic money to the church. I say the devil has had it long enough, right Reverend?!"

Thad tried to join in with the frantic cheerfulness. But there were too many unanswered questions for Thad Larkin to be happy. A feeling of anxiety and hopelessness coursed through him. Events were out of control. Somehow, he knew there would be more killings in Creekside, Arizona, and he had no idea how to stop it.

Chapter Seven

Rebecca Torveen laughed uncontrollably. "I can't believe it! Say that again, Brother!"

Wes pretended to be angry. "I said, when we pull up at the Creekside General Store, I'm gonna go next door to Sally's Dress Shop. I wanna buy somethin' there."

Rebecca laughed again and threw out words that were overwhelmed by the clattering of a buckboard and the pounding hooves of four horses. As he watched her, Wes realized his little sister, now twenty-one, had grown into a lovely young woman, as Maddie had done. Rebecca's reddish brown hair surrounded a face with vibrant green eyes, a large forehead and a perfectly proportioned mouth and nose. A small collection of freckles dotted her nose.

Maddie and Rebecca had been friends since their time in school together and Wes was certain his sister would be happy when she learned about the wedding to take place the next day. But he fought the temptation to confide in her about the wonderful change Maddie had brought into his life. Rebecca was good at many things, but keeping a secret was not one of them.

The Torveens were perched on the spring seat of the buckboard, Rebecca sitting between her two brothers. Owen tried to smile and look happy as he guided the horses. His sister had been joyful since Wes's arrival. She seemed to accept unconditionally that Wes had only killed men in self-defense. Owen wondered if all those childhood memories of Wes being harassed and bullied had blinded her to the One Arm Savage Wes had become.

Owen cared little for Rob Laverty but he had to admit the sheriff was right about one thing. Wes could outdraw any man in town. Unless he was ambushed, Wes would certainly take down Laverty, Stanley Wiggins and Ed Horton. And would it stop there? There were others in town who had picked on Wes, though less aggressively.

The One Arm Savage had to be stopped. Surely, the three men in ambush could do the job. All he'd have to do was make sure his brother was standing alone on the buckboard. Set him up as a target. Rebecca would never suspect his involvement.

"Say, Brother, can't yuh get these nags to move any faster?"

"I'll try, Wes," Owen shouted. "Sure hate for you to be late to Sally's Dress Shop!"

As both his sister and brother guffawed, Owen did note that Wes had been unusually good tempered that morning. Maybe killing Josh Franklin and Blake Crowley had improved his disposition.

Rebecca and Wes continued to laugh and chide each other. Neither one noticed the grim look in Owen's eyes. There was another reason Owen had to go along with murdering his brother, a reason which had nothing to do with saving lives. As his siblings laughed, Owen pressed his lips together and whipped the horses to move faster.

Sheriff Laverty lay on the roof of the Rome Saloon and checked his timepiece. The Torveens should be arriving any time now.

"Fortune is smiling on you, Rob Laverty," he mused aloud. After all, before leaving town, Doc Stamford had told him that he and the preacher were riding out to the Brent place where Dean Ochs was kicking up dust. Good. The doctor and the preacher were two men who could have hindered his plan.

Still, Laverty was tense, and not only because he was about to ambush a man: a man he couldn't face in an honest gunfight. There would be three guns firing at Wes Torveen but Sheriff Rob Laverty had to be the man who got the credit for bringing down the One Arm Savage. The sheriff craved recognition and fame. Now was his chance.

Of course, he couldn't get what he wanted by telling the truth. No newspaper or magazine would make him look good for pulling off an ambush. He had already concocted a good story. Getting the others to go along might be difficult but he'd think of something.

The fine looking wagon entered town and began to move toward the Creekside General Store. Owen and Rebecca Torveen had made a success of what had once been a hardscrabble ranch and could now afford the best.

As the buckboard stopped in front of the general store and Owen applied the brake, Laverty noted something strange about Wes Torveen. The gunfighter looked relaxed and even happy. The strange quickly became bizarre. As Rebecca and Owen entered the general store, Wes darted into Sally's Dress Shop.

"What the hell?" Rob Laverty whispered to himself. His eyes slithered from one store window to the next. Inside the Creekside General Store, Owen and Rebecca were talking with Jonah Frazier, the owner. There was no mistaking Jonah, a large man with a handle bar mustache.

Next door, Sally Mercer was removing a gingham dress from the shop's window display. This time the sheriff limited his mutterings to "hell."

Wes came out of the shop, carefully carrying a long but obviously light box. He placed it under the seat of the wagon and then entered the general store. About ten minutes later, Wes Torveen exited the Creekside General Store, leaving the door wide open. He jumped onto the wagon where he stood on the bed and gave his brother a friendly shout. He obviously expected Owen to toss him some items from the store.

The sheriff smirked as he aimed his Winchester. Wes Torveen was showing off what he could do with just one arm. Rob Laverty would remind the gunfighter that pride comes before the fall.

Laverty squeezed the trigger of his rifle. Wes Torveen jerked violently and staggered but remained on his feet. He drew his pearl handled six shooter and returned fire. The bullet hit close by Laverty, forcing him to roll as he levered the Winchester and got off a second shot which went wild.

From between the batwings of the Rome Saloon, Ed Horton fired twice in Wes Torveen's direction. Torveen jumped off the wagon as he sent a flame into the saloon. Horton spun, stumbled out into the street and collapsed. Wes took cover under the wagon as Stanley Wiggins fired from the alley beside the saloon.

Rebecca Torveen screamed as Wes's body convulsed from the shot. Instinctively, she began to run toward her wounded brother but was stopped when the store owner grabbed her arm.

"Don't go out there, Miss Rebecca," Jonah Frazier shouted. "You'll get hurt."

The young woman struggled with Frazier as he

forced her behind the counter. "I've got to help Wes!"

Owen Torveen silently cursed as he watched the ambush unfold. Stanley Wiggins's shot propelled harmlessly into the air. Wiggins had been terrified by the sight of Ed Horton getting shot. The bartender was now retreating into the shadows of the alley, becoming a bystander. What had been intended as a quick ambush could now turn into a standoff.

"Get down, Miss Rebecca, please!" Frazier had maneuvered the young woman behind the counter and was forcing her to crouch down.

The street was now empty of people. Noticing where Wes was positioned under the wagon, Owen got an idea to end the standoff and make himself appear as a man determined to help his brother. He turned and ran toward the store's counter, hastily grabbing the Sharpes Fifty he knew was under it.

"Keep her safe, Jonah!" He yelled at the storekeeper who now had Rebecca kneeling on the floor.

Running back to the door, Owen drew his Smith and Wesson from its shoulder holster and hurled a bullet in the direction of the Rome Saloon but nowhere close to Rob Laverty. With the sheriff's eyes on him, Owen jumped off the boardwalk and did a fast crawl to his brother's side.

"Do you know how many there are?" Owen asked as he lay beside his brother.

"With Ed Horton dead or dyin' there's only two," Wes replied. "Wiggins is in the alley, and Creekside's keeper of law and order is on the roof."

Owen placed his Smith and Wesson beside Wes. "Use this while you're reloading," he patted the rifle. "I'm going on top of the wagon, can get off some good shots from there."

"No, Owen! Yuh'd be a sittin' duck!"

"Don't worry, little brother. Haven't my notions about helping you out always worked in the past?"

Wes gave his brother a kindly smile. "Guess they have at that."

"OK. Keep our good sheriff busy for me."

"Will do, and Owen, thanks."

Wes picked up the Smith and Wesson and fired three successive shots at Laverty. The sheriff once again found himself rolling on the roof in a desperate act of self-preservation.

Confident that he had his brother's trust, Owen jumped onto the wagon and hurried to sit down on the seat. He released the brake. The horses, terrified by the shooting, lurched forward. A horrifying cry of pain cut the air as a back wheel of the wagon ran over Wes Torveen.

Rob Laverty watched all this from his position across the street. He stared in wonderment at the crushed figure on the ground. Wes Torveen's arm was moving up and down as if beckoning for help.

Laverty took careful aim and fired. Torveen's arm dropped to the ground.

The sheriff smiled at the gruesome sight. He was the lawman who had brought down the One Arm Savage.

Chapter Eight

Thad Larkin stood in his office speaking to the Lord. He gave an amen to his prayer for wisdom and patience, then, Bible in hand, he left the office and immediately encountered a need for both of the attributes he had requested.

"Jonah, I've already explained the decision."

Jonah Frazier's face was red as he paced about nervously. The storeowner and Thad were the only two men in the church, though a crowd was waiting outside. "Preacher, you gotta understand. We've got the body of a famous outlaw in our town. It's the chance of a lifetime. We hafta show the body for a week or two. It's the only decent thing to do."

"Rebecca and Owen want to bury their brother today."

"You could talk 'em out of it, Preacher! Tell 'em 'bout how the whole town would benefit. Folks would come here from miles 'round. The eating places, the hotel and most of the stores would get extra business. Quote 'em something from the Bible."

"No, Jonah."

"Look, I'll see to it the church gets ten per cent of the profits—"

"No, Jonah!"

The storeowner made a deep sigh and, head down, walked out of the church a defeated man. Reverend Larkin felt the need for another prayer, or did he just want to delay the obligation in front of him? He couldn't be sure.

The pastor left the church. Outside was a large gathering of people, all of them facing an approaching buckboard. The wagon stopped in front of the crowd. Rebecca and Owen were seated at the front. Wes Torveen's coffin rested on the bed.

Thad exchanged nods with Owen and the buckboard moved slowly toward the town's cemetery, which was a short distance from the church. Thad led the crowd walking behind the buckboard. The procession sang *Shall We Gather by the River*.

There was no fence surrounding the long, flat field which served as Creekside's cemetery, only a wide path which cut through the middle. Owen guided the buckboard about half way down the path and then stopped. He stepped down from the wagon and helped his sister off. Thad and Brad Myers, the ranch's foreman, joined Owen and the three men lifted Wes's coffin off the wagon and carried it to where a freshly dug grave awaited.

The coffin now lay beside the grim cavity and the crowd began to form a circle around it, allowing space for Reverend Larkin to stand at the front of the grave. As people settled in, Thad noticed that Brad Myers stood on one side of

Rebecca and held her hand. Rumors of a romance between Rebecca and her ranch foreman had bounced about Creekside for months. Hardly surprising: Brad was a handsome, sandy haired man of average height with a strong, muscular build. Rebecca gave a sorrowful smile to both Brad and Owen who stood on the other side of her. With her free hand, Rebecca caressed a small wooden cross that hung on a green ribbon around her neck. The previous day, Rebecca had told Thad the cross had been made for her many years before by Wes.

Larkin began the service, "Many of you that are gathered here this afternoon knew Wes Torveen as a boy—"

"Killers!" Maddie Johnson's voice screeched through the crowd like the whine of a bullet. She stood on the opposite side of the open grave from Owen Torveen and pointed an accusing finger at him. "You carried Wes's body here in the same buckboard you used to kill him!"

Owen held out a hand toward the young woman. "That's not true."

"Yes, it is!"

Owen closed his eyes briefly before trying again. "Maddie, I already explained to you, Wes and I made a quick plan. He was to stay between the wheels of the buckboard and I would drive over him. Then, he would jump into the bed and I'd drive him out of town. The plan was desperate, but it might have worked. Wes must have become confused about where he was and a wheel ran over him."

Rebecca spoke softly. "I'm sure Owen is telling the truth."

"He's lying!" Maddie yelled as she made her hand into a claw and thrust it toward Owen Torveen.

Screams and gasps exploded from the crowd as Owen collapsed and the top half of his body lay dangling over the open grave. Brad Myers grabbed his boss and tried to help him to his feet but Owen's legs were rubber.

"Maddie . . . please . . . no!" The brave stoicism that had dominated Rebecca's face vanished. The corner of her eyes dampened and her voice wavered with fear. "Owen would never have hurt Wes, Owen loved his brother."

"I loved him too!" Maddie shot back, her voice laced with loss and confusion. "We were going to ask Reverend Larkin to marry us after the service this morning."

"That's crazy!" Brad Myers exclaimed. Myers now had his boss sitting upright on the ground.

"No," Thad Larkin spoke calmly. The crowd looked at him in surprise, as if they had forgotten his presence. "From what I hear, Wes bought a gingham dress shortly before he was killed. No one understood why. Now, we do. The dress was for Maddie to wear on her wedding day."

Maddie Johnson lowered her head and, for a moment, her agonized cry was all that was heard at the gravesite. The young woman then looked up and gazed at Owen Torveen. "I remember how you use to stand up for Wes . . . guess what happened yesterday was an accident."

Maddie moved her hand in front of her, across her chest. Owen Torveen stood up and brushed himself off. He and Brad Myers returned to their places beside Rebecca.

A fire suddenly raged in Maddie's eyes as she looked about the crowd. That fire blazed with increased ferocity as she looked at Rob Laverty and Stanley Wiggins. The two men were standing together behind most of the mourners. They seemed to be doing everything they could to be invisible.

"I'm glad Wes killed Ed Horton," Maddie's voice sounded lower and more intimidating. "And very soon Wes will kill the other two men who ambushed him."

Thad Larkin glanced at Agatha and Dencel Burke who stood behind their niece. They both looked stunned, terrified and helpless. The pastor decided to try and intervene.

"Maddie, I sympathize with your grief but—"

"I'm speaking the truth, Reverend Larkin!" Maddie Johnson half closed her eyes and raised her right hand to her shoulder. "Like Lazarus, Wes Torveen will rise from the dead and walk this earth again. He will take revenge on his murderers; only then will his spirit find peace."

"I ain't no murderer!" The sheriff's eyes avoided Maddie as he spoke. "You folks all know what Wes Torveen was doing. He'd already killed two men. So, I got up a posse and went after him. Ed Horton and Stanley Wiggins had been sworn in as deputies. It was all legal like."

"You're standing at a graveside, Rob Laverty, take your hat off."

Maddie delivered the mundane request in a voice heavy with threat. Laverty yanked off his Stetson.

"Today, we bury the only man I could ever love. Soon, Rob Laverty and Stanley Wiggins will by lying in this same field." Maddie Johnson lowered her hand and her eyes opened wide. "I'm sorry, Reverend Larkin. Please go ahead with the service."

Larkin paused and then followed the request. But every word he spoke sounded hollow. The pastor felt no one was listening to him. Everyone seemed to be reflecting on Maddie Johnson's prophecy.

After the formalities were over, nobody left. The citizens of Creekside wanted to watch Wes Torveen's coffin lowered into the ground and see the many shovels of dirt piled on it, as if to keep it in place.

Chapter Nine

Stanley Wiggins escorted the last of his customers out the batwing doors of the Shooting Star Saloon. The two men were drunk and feisty. One of them turned back as he stepped onto the boardwalk outside. "Jus' maybe Pete an' me don't wanna leave yet!"

The barkeep replied firmly. "And just maybe the owners of this establishment will decide you ain't welcome here—ever!"

"Come on, Fred," the other drunk spoke in a self-righteous manner. "Let's go complain to the mayor 'bout hows we've been treated."

They staggered off as Stanley closed the door in front of the batwings and locked it. The bartender gave a sigh of fatigue as he went through the Shooting Star turning off the kerosene lights that were attached to the walls.

Wiggins had been shaken by Maddie Johnson's threats at Wes Torveen's funeral. But now his attitude toward the afternoon events was downright whimsical. Why, watching Wes get buried had worked up a strong thirst in a lot of men. Sundays were usually a quiet time for the Shooting Star, but not this Sunday. Counting the loot would be a real pleasure.

Two lights were still burning, both of them

behind the bar. Those lights always stayed on until Stanley took the cashbox and locked it in the safe. The bartender bellowed out *Shall We Gather at the River* in a mocking voice as he sauntered behind the bar. He then complimented his own wit, "Those church folks are all fools."

"Evenin', Stanley."

The bartender gasped and looked around. He couldn't see anyone, but then darkness shrouded most of the saloon. Wiggins decided his imagination had become inflamed by recent events. He began to do a check of the materials under the bar as he did every night before putting away the cashbox. The familiar routine brought him some comfort.

But not for long. "Evenin', Stanley." A figure stepped into the murky patch of light cast by the lamps behind the bar.

Stanley Wiggins brought his right hand to his face as if shielding his eyes against what stood in front of them. "Wes Torveen!" The bartender spoke in a high pitched whisper. "We buried you hours ago."

"That's right, Stanley. I saw yuh standin' near my graveside along with my other chums. Yuh fellas were sharin' a chuckle or two. After all these years, I can still provide my friends with a good laugh."

"We wasn't laughing at you, Wes—"

"Then who was yuh laughin' at? Maddie, who was in grief?"

"No, Wes, no, it was that . . . ah . . . preacher."

"He read from the good book. What's funny 'bout that?"

"Nothing," Stanley was confused and terrified. He moved his hand toward the .44 that was kept under the bar.

"So, I guess you fellas was havin' one more laugh on Wes Torveen."

Desperation prodded Wiggins into a reckless move. "Let me explain, Wes. All I'm asking for is just a minute or two of your time."

"Why, sure." Wes Torveen lifted his left arm in a "go ahead" gesture.

Stanley grabbed the .44, but in his nervousness, slammed his hand against the edge of the bar as he brought the gun up. He yelled a loud curse. Those were his final words. A bullet from Torveen's gun cut into the bartender's chest. Stanley Wiggins fell to the floor.

The bartender writhed in pain as he listened to footsteps slowly walking around the bar and then looked up to see the man who had just shot him. Wes Torveen gave a loud mocking laugh. "Now it's my turn to have the chuckles, Stanley. I got one more little joke to play, hope yuh live long enough to see it."

Torveen reached into a side pocket of his frock coat and brought out a piece of cloth. He crouched over Stanley Wiggins and dangled the piece of gingham in his face. "Right pretty cloth, don't yuh think?"

A gurgling sound came out of the bartender's throat as blood oozed out the side of his mouth and began to stain his chin.

"This cloth was torn from the dress I was gonna give to Maddie for her weddin' day. Only there ain't gonna be no weddin' day. Not since my old pals murdered me. So, here, Stanley, this is for you."

He dropped the piece of cloth onto the bartender. Stanley Wiggins gave no response. He'd never respond to anything again.

There was a loud pounding at the door. Sheriff Rob Laverty shouted from outside, "Stanley, you in there?"

The One Arm Savage stood up and looked at the door with anticipation. "Well, well, looks like the party is jus' gettin' started."

Chapter Ten

"Try again, Laverty!" A few stray pieces of tobacco flew from Fenton Stamford's mouth as he made his demand.

Rob Laverty took a deep breath. He knew the mayor didn't like him and was working to have him ousted from his job.

The sheriff again pounded on the locked door of the Shooting Star. "I don't think there's anyone there, Mr. Mayor. Stanley's probably gone home for the night."

Stamford glanced at the saloon's window where a pulled down shade blocked any view from outside. "You could be right, but two drunk saddle bums came by my house . . . oh . . . twenty minutes ago, and complained about Stanley throwing them out of the saloon."

"You got all worked up 'cause of two barflies?!"

The doctor briefly touched the pistol strapped around his waist. "This town has been through some very strange days, and some very bizarre ideas can get into people's heads. Thought I should come by and see if Stanley needed help. On my way, I thought I heard a shot coming from inside the Shooting Star. I spotted you and thought you might help. Guess my brain is getting pretty tired."

Laverty ignored the barb. "The noise you heard was probably a shot fired at the sky by some drunk Stanley had pushed out the back door."

Fenton pushed his hat back a few inches and scratched his head. "You may be right . . . still . . . I hate to do this, but better safe than sorry." He pulled out a set of keys, separated one and opened the door of the saloon. "Give the place a careful look: office, basement, the works. Let me know what you find. I need to get back to my house. I have a patient there."

The sheriff's eyes rose with astonishment and anger. "You never told me 'bout those keys!"

"That's right."

"Why didn't you just open up in the first place, instead of making me pound on the door?"

"Like I just told you, Laverty, I don't like using the keys. A man should be careful about opening the properties of other people."

"Why don't you let me have those keys?"

Fenton Stamford gave the sheriff a look conveying suspicion and contempt. "I'll be at my house." He quickly turned and walked away.

The sheriff gritted his teeth and said nothing. He only had a little more time of putting up with the likes of Fenton Stamford. Soon, stories of the man who killed the One Arm Savage would be everywhere. Rob Laverty would be a hero, and heroes don't have to tolerate fools.

The sheriff pushed through the bat wings and noted the lights that were still on behind the bar. "Stanley—you here?"

Laverty moved cautiously toward the bar; even so, he collided with several chairs. The lights did little to help.

When he got behind the bar, however, he had a clear view of the corpse of Stanley Wiggins. The lawman inhaled and took a step back as if death were a disease that could be transmitted.

He slowly stepped toward the body and crouched over it, picking up a piece of fabric that lay on the corpse. "Looks like it came from that dress Sally Mercer had in her shop. The dress Wes Torveen bought."

Laverty dropped the fabric as his throat went tight. What he heard next caused his entire body to tremble.

"You're out late tonight, Sheriff. Need to get yuh some rest. I hear yuh got some busy days comin'."

Laverty slowly moved out of his crouch. He was now standing behind the bar facing the open door of the Shooting Star. A figure was standing in the doorway, in front of the batwings.

"Who are you?" The lawman tried to sound tough but his voice wobbled.

The man in the doorway spoke mockingly. "Yuh should recognize me, Robbie. I heard 'bout yuh sendin' a telegram to the Denver Post, tellin' that important paper 'bout how yuh brought down the One Arm Savage."

"Wes Torveen." Laverty spoke in a whisper.

"Yep, Rob, I'm here to do you a favor."

"What kind of favor?"

"Why, I'm gonna give yuh a chance to kill me again. Jus' think how impressed those folks at the Denver Post will be when they find out yuh killed the One Arm Savage twice."

Rob Laverty tried to laugh. It came out as a sob.

"Let's step out in the street, Rob, find out how fast yuh really are."

Laverty pounded his fist on the bar and screamed at the man in the doorway. "You go back to hell or wherever you demons come from! Leave me alone, Wes Torveen, leave me alone!"

Rob Laverty began to cry uncontrollably. He rested his head on the bar and put both arms over it. He refused to look up, like a child hiding under a blanket, hoping the boogieman would disappear.

But he could hear the voice that continued to taunt him. "I see yuh don't feel up to a fair fight right yet. Don't worry. I'm a patient man. I'll be waitin'."

Laverty continued to keep his head down for several minutes after the voice ceased. When he finally raised his eyes, all he could see was a vacant doorway made blurry by the tears that cluttered his vision.

Chapter Eleven

Ellen Brent worked her hands nervously. Her face was still damp from tears. "You've done so much for us already, Reverend Larkin. I feel awful unloading my problems on you like this; the doctor shouldn't have gone for you."

The pastor patted the Bible he had just read a psalm from. "I'm not the one you're taking your troubles to, Ellen."

Ellen Brent and Thad Larkin were sitting in the living room of Fenton Stamford's house, occupying the two most comfortable chairs in Creekside. The living room also served as a waiting room. Stamford was attending to Tommy who was sleeping in the area of the house Fenton called his surgery.

"It was good of the doctor to let Tommy and me stay here tonight."

"Fenton is a good guy."

The woman managed a smile. "I don't know what I would have done if we had been in the hotel when Tommy started screaming in his sleep. He started doing that after his father died. The problem seemed to have stopped, but with everything that has happened these last few days . . ."

"Tommy will be fine once you get resettled in Denver."

"I hope so," Ellen pressed her lips together for a moment and then continued. "Tommy didn't want me to sell the farm and, in a way, I didn't want to. I could have hired some men and run the place myself, but it wouldn't have been the same without Tom. Every day I would have been reminded of what we planned together."

The woman's anxiety was prodding her to repeat matters they had already discussed in detail. Reverend Larkin decided on a diversion. "What stage is your brother coming in on tomorrow?"

"The morning one," she replied. "We'll be leaving in the afternoon. William needs a bookkeeper for his mining company and Tommy and I need a new life."

Thad smiled and nodded his head, hoping his face didn't betray his emotions. The two months following Tom Brent's death had also been hard on the pastor. He found himself attracted to Ellen and thinking about what could happen once she was over her grief.

But Ellen needed a pastor, not a potential suitor. Thad had filled that role and had tried to appear supportive over her decision to move to Denver. Sending her off tomorrow would not be easy. *Never mind what might have been,* Larkin thought.

Ellen looked up anxiously as Fenton stepped out of his surgery, walked across a small hallway and entered the living room. "How is he doing, Doctor?"

"Just fine." Stamford gave the woman a comforting smile. "I was hesitant to give such a young boy laudanum but the dose was small. He's sleeping well and his breathing is regular. Now, Tommy isn't the only one who needs rest, I suggest you—"

The front door flew open, banged against a wall, and coasted partially back to its original place. Rob Laverty didn't bother closing it. He ran toward the doctor and began to look around the room as if trying to spot hidden enemies.

The doctor was incensed. "Laverty, I told you to report to me, not to stampede in like a wild donkey!"

"You wouldn't be acting so high and mighty if you'd seen what I did, Mr. Mayor!"

"What do you mean?"

"Wes Torveen: he's out to kill me."

"Nonsense," the doctor shot back. "Wes Torveen is dead."

"I'm telling you, I jus' saw him and he's out to kill me!"

Laverty spotted the pastor, and took three quick steps toward him. "Preacher, you gotta talk to her."

Thad looked confused as he stood up. The sheriff obviously wasn't referring to Ellen Brent. "Talk to whom?"

"Maddie Johnson!" The lawman's eyes widened with desperation. "You heard what she said at Wes's funeral . . . well . . . it's come true. That girl really is a witch! She brought the One Arm Savage back to life. He just killed Stanley Wiggins. And he left a piece of cloth on Stanley's body . . . gingham . . . from the dress he bought for Maddie. Talk to Maddie Johnson, Preacher, make her take the curse off; she's made a pact with the devil!"

"Mom."

"That's Tommy." Ellen quickly rose from her chair and ran into the surgery.

"Now look what you've done, Laverty!" Fenton Stamford's face was red and his body quivering with anger. "I've always thought you were an incompetent sheriff and now you've proven it. Tomorrow I'm calling a special meeting of the town council to have you relieved of your duties."

Rob Laverty shouted a curse; his right hand moved downward toward his holstered gun. Thad tackled the lawman. As they went down, Laverty managed to grab his pistol. He skimmed the .45 across Thad's head moments after they hit the floor.

The sheriff scrambled up and ran out the still open front door. Larkin weaved back onto his feet and started to pursue the lawman.

"Stop." The doctor placed a firm hand on

Larkin's shoulder. "You could have a concussion!"

"Not even close," Thad replied. "I was able to duck most of the blow. We've got to stop that mad man."

"Yes, but not unarmed; give me a second." The doctor strode to a closet beside the surgery and brought out the holster and gun he had worn earlier. In his other hand was a Henry.

Stamford spoke in short bursts as he handed the rifle to Thad and began to strap on his own weapon. "Laverty really believes a ghost is after him. He's probably heading for his office. He'll feel safer there. Thank goodness the streets are mostly empty. That fool could shoot anyone he sees. Let's move fast but make it quiet."

The two men left the house, walking quickly but cautiously. The doctor's house was set several yards back from the main road.

The roar of two shots overwhelmed the soft crunch of their footsteps. Both men began to run toward the sheriff's office, the moon and stars providing their only light.

As they sped down the main street, both men noted that there were no other people in sight. But, as they passed the Shooting Star Saloon they spotted a dark bulge in the middle of the street.

Thad and the doctor crouched over the body of Rob Laverty. Larkin laid the Henry down, pulled a match from his pocket and struck it off his thumbnail. The clergyman quickly looked around and saw no movements that might indicate that the killer was close by.

Fenton Stamford spoke without emotion as he examined the body. "He's gone. Both bullets got him in the chest." The doctor picked up a piece of cloth from Laverty's forehead. "Gingham," was all Stamford said.

Thad turned his head back slightly, taking a careful look at the Shooting Star. "There seems to be a slight glow around the shade in the saloon's window."

"I didn't notice that before. Maybe Stanley forgot to turn off the back lights when he closed."

Thad shook his head as he blew out the flame and tossed the matchstick aside. "I don't think so. I believe Laverty was telling us at least part of the truth. Don't like to say this, but I think Stanley Wiggins's corpse is lying inside the Shooting Star with a piece of gingham cloth on top of it."

Stamford closed his eyes and muttered a few curses. When his eyelids were up again he stared directly at the pastor. "Everyone in Creekside knows that Maddie Johnson claimed she'd bring back Wes Torveen to kill Laverty and Wiggins. Now, if you're right, both men have been murdered. This town is going to go crazy."

Thad grimaced and gave a deep sigh. "We need to find a new sheriff and get to the truth soon."

"You're right." Fenton took the badge off

Laverty's chest and held it out to Thad Larkin.

Reverend Larkin looked nervously at the object. "I'm a minister of the Gospel, not a lawman."

"You used to be a lawman, and from what I hear, a very good one."

"I have a different calling now."

"This town is in big trouble: trouble that can't be solved from a pulpit. I know how you feel, Thad. But right now your calling is to bring a killer to justice before this town burns Maddie Johnson at the stake for being a witch."

Thad Larkin stared at the badge.

Chapter Twelve

Thad Larkin put down his right hand and removed his left from the Bible being held by Fenton Stamford in his capacity as Creekside's mayor.

"Congratulations, Sheriff Larkin." There was no celebration in Stamford's voice. "And God speed."

There were a few awkward minutes as Larkin shook hands with two of Creekside's business-men and its only lawyer. The three men constituted the members of the town council besides the mayor. They were all members of the Creekside Community Church and still referred to Thad as "Preacher" before leaving the office.

After they left, the new sheriff and the doctor stood silently in the sheriff's office. Stamford broke the silence. "I thought I'd wait until Ellen and Tommy left on the stage before swearing you in."

"I appreciate that."

"Her brother seems to be a fine man."

"Yes."

"I'm sure Ellen and Tommy will have a good life in Denver."

"Yes."

The doctor's voice dropped an octave or so lower. "There is a problem, though."

"What's that?"

"Well, as you know, matters got pretty crazy in my house last night. Tommy overheard things. Apparently, the boy told some folks all about the two murders."

Larkin shrugged his shoulders. "People would know about that anyway."

"Yes, but Tommy filled in the details. He told some people all about Laverty claiming to have seen the ghost of Wes Torveen and the cloths from the gingham dress. If the whole town doesn't know about it by now it soon will. Ellen apologized for the boy—"

"Ellen Brent doesn't need to apologize for anything."

"Of course," the doctor replied immediately.

Thad Larkin drummed his fingers on the one desk in the office; it looked almost identical to a desk he had often stood behind in his first job as a lawman. A nightmare he had kept locked up broke out and flooded his thoughts.

Thad Larkin had been nineteen when he became sheriff of Pemberton, Arizona, after serving for one year as a deputy. His first few months had been difficult with the usual assortment of barflies and saddle tramps testing out the new sheriff. But he quickly proved up to the job and the testing stopped.

Thad usually went easy on men who sold

tanglefoot. The sellers of homemade liquor were mostly poor people doing what they could to survive. Zeke Emhurst and his two boys were an exception. Zeke's tanglefoot had blinded one man and put another in the grave. All of Zeke's liquor may not have been that destructive but the sheriff wasn't risking it. Thad had ridden out to Zeke's dilapidated cabin and talked with him and his oldest son, Gill.

Both men had initially appeared old and wasted, though with a careful look, Thad pegged Gill at around sixteen. Like his father, Gill was thin with a gaunt, unshaven face. And like his father, Gill wore a large, wide brimmed hat. The one time Larkin had seen him in town, the younger brother, Jess, had worn a similar hat. It seemed to be the family's one tradition.

"I'm closing you down, Zeke," Larkin's voice was a matter of fact monotone. "If I hear about you selling jugs out here or if you try selling in town, I'll arrest you, understand?"

"Yup."

"How about you, Gill?"

"Unnerstand."

"Where's your other boy, Zeke?"

" 'Round somewhere's."

"How old is Jess anyway?"

"Old enough not ta be scared by no tin star."

"You tell him what I said, Zeke. This family is through selling tanglefoot."

"OK, Sheriff, now if yo're done speakin' yore piece why don't ya just ride out."

One week later Boone Conklin stormed into the sheriff's office. "Zeke Emhurst and his two boys are in town, Thad. They're behind the livery. They musta given ol' Amos a free jug to allow them to set up shop there. Them Emhursts are breaking the law!"

Larkin ran a hand across his face to hide a smirk. Boone was the owner of the town's largest saloon. His outrage over the law being violated sprouted from economic soil.

The lawman was nevertheless sincere when he thanked Boone for the information. "I'll get over there right now."

Boone Conklin returned to his saloon and Thad began a quick walk toward Murphy's Livery. The front double doors of the livery stood open but Thad didn't see anyone as he stepped inside and glanced around for the owner.

"Amos is probably off somewhere enjoying that jug," Larkin whispered. "The fool, I hope the stuff doesn't kill him."

Voices came from behind the building. "I ain't sellin' ya a jug 'til ya pay me fer last time."

"Look, I'm a man who needs a drink."

"Ya git nothin' 'til ya pay."

"I'll show you!"

There was no back door to the livery. Thad hurried out the front. He didn't see the figure emerge from a shadowed corner of the building and quietly follow him.

The lawman ran to the back of the livery where he saw Bert Smith, a town drunk, standing with his hand over an ancient pistol which nestled in a cracked and torn holster. Bert was facing Zeke and Gill Emhurst, who were positioned near an old buckboard with a bed full of jugs. The Emhursts were not wearing iron but Gill was edging closer to his scattergun which stood propped against the back wall of the livery.

"I'm warnin' you and your boy, Zeke! You give me one of them jugs, else I draw on you."

Smith's entire body was shaking. Larkin approached the alcoholic from behind and yanked his gun from its holster. The sheriff hastily checked the pistol which was empty. That didn't surprise Thad. When Bert Smith got ahold of some money he didn't spend it on ammunition.

"Get out of here, Bert." Larkin handed Smith his pistol.

"I need me a drink."

"You'll have to wait until tonight," the lawman replied. Bert worked as a swamper at Boone Conklin's saloon. Part of his pay came in liquid form.

"You don't unnerstand, Sheriff." Bert managed to get the pistol back into its holster.

"Go home, Bert."

Smith's voice became a whine. "I ain't got no home."

"Leave!"

Bert followed the lawman's orders, mumbling curses. While he was talking with Smith, Thad had been watching Zeke and Gill. Both men knew the sheriff was there to arrest them. Their eyes brimmed with hate and determination.

Gill took slow and clumsy steps toward the scattergun. A dissolute life had given his motions an erratic quality.

"Stop right there, Gill," Larkin ordered. "Don't move."

Both Gill and Zeke had a distant look in their eyes as if looking past the sheriff. Thad remembered Conklin saying, "Zeke Emhurst and his *two* boys are in town."

Thad glanced behind him and saw Jess Emhurst standing at the corner of the livery with a rifle pointed at him. The lawman hit the ground and rolled as the Winchester fired.

Larkin drew his Colt. He knew Gill was going for his scattergun. He had to take out Jess quickly. The lawman fired two shots into the younger Emhurst who twirled, losing his grip on the Winchester before dropping to the ground. A high pitched cry came from the fallen youth whose body twitched then went completely still.

Larkin swerved his Colt toward Gill who now

had the scattergun in hand. Thad pumped a bullet into Gill's leg, who tossed the gun in his father's direction as he went down. The gun skittered along the ground but stopped a few feet from Zeke, who now stood like a man stunned.

The sheriff scrambled to his feet taking a quick look at Jess who still lay motionless on the ground. "Stay right where you are, Zeke!" Holding his Colt in his right hand, Larkin moved quickly to the shotgun and scooped it up with his left.

"What kind o' man are ya, Tin Star?"

"A man who does his job."

"Does that mean pullin' down on women folks?" Zeke roared. He had to in order to be heard above Gill who was thrashing about on the ground yelling in pain.

Larkin roared back. "What are you talking about?"

Zeke's face contorted with anguish and desperation. "Ya shot down my little girl, Jessie."

"Wha—" Holstering his pistol Thad ran to the still body that lay near the corner of the livery. He crouched beside the body, picked up the wrist and felt for a pulse that wasn't there.

Slowly, Larkin lifted the large, wide brimmed hat. A cascade of beautiful brown hair splayed over the ground. The face reflected the ravages of undernourishment, but even so it was lovely and it was the face of a child.

"Ya ain't nothin' but a killer, Tin Star, a yella belly who kills little girls." The voice came from only a few feet away.

Thad lay down the shotgun and stood, facing Zeke Emhurst. "You had the whole town thinking Jess was a boy about Gill's age. Why?!"

"I need to protect myself. People leave ya alone when they reckon on two strong boys." Emhurst took a few steps back. Something in Larkin's eyes conveyed a threat.

"How old was Jessie?"

"Ten. Not that it's any o' yore business."

Loud shouts from a distance blended with Gill's painful cries providing a bizarre cacophony of sound which Larkin ignored. "You let a child hide in that livery with a gun. You told her to shoot anyone who caused you trouble. What kind of man are you, Zeke?!"

"I ain't no killer!" Emhurst yelled. "You're the one that fired into Jessie. Now, who's gonna cook and clean for my boy and me?"

Larkin slammed a fist into Zeke's face. The man hit the ground and began to moan even louder than his son.

"Get up, Zeke!"

Zeke Emhurst couldn't or wouldn't obey the lawman's command, leaving Thad Larkin feeling strangely helpless. He wanted desperately to hit Zeke again, to beat the man until he was near death.

Larkin turned and almost stumbled as he once again approached the corpse. He dropped onto his knees beside Jessie's body.

Moments later, a group of armed men arrived at the scene to investigate the shots. They found their sheriff weeping uncontrollably.

Thad resigned as sheriff the next day. He began to travel the country and read a lot. He ended up in an eastern college studying to be a pastor. But Larkin knew that once his schooling was over he would have to return to the west. Arizona was his future.

Larkin learned about the opening at the Creekside Community Church as his final year of school ended. He accepted the position through the mail. When he had his first meeting with the church's deacons he didn't recognize Fenton Stamford, but the doctor recognized him.

"This office bring back some bad memories?" Stamford asked.

"Yes. You're the only one in town who knows about my past; let's keep it that way."

"Sure," Fenton replied. "You had some bad luck back then. I just happened to be in Pemberton, visiting a friend. You were the talk of the town. I saw you getting on the stage, waving good-bye to everyone. I've never seen a man who looked so miserable."

"I'm feeling pretty miserable now," Larkin

said. "Remember, I'm only taking this job on a temporary basis."

"I'll remember."

"And I'll still preach on Sunday morning."

"That was our agreement, and you can hire one deputy. Laverty never could find a deputy willing to work with him more than a couple of weeks." Fenton tried to smile and half succeeded. "You've become a spiritual man and you have a spiritual job: find out who killed Stanley Wiggins and Rob Laverty."

"What's so spiritual about that?"

The doctor's smile broadened. "You have to prove it all wasn't done by the ghost of a gunslinger brought back to life by a witch."

Chapter Thirteen

After Fenton Stamford left the office, Thad did a quick check of the place and found nothing unusual. The gun rack on the wall held two rifles: one Winchester and one Henry. Both were well cared for.

There was a door that led to three jail cells and a back door that led to one privy. Returning to his desk, Larkin gave some thought to what Dr. Stamford had said about his "spiritual job."

The new sheriff of Creekside, Arizona was certain that many people in the town believed the ghost of Wes Torveen had killed two men and that Wes's return from the grave had been instigated by a curse from Maddie Johnson. "Faith always has to battle superstition," Thad spoke aloud to himself. "And faith doesn't always seem to win."

The sheriff laughed softly. "You're not a preacher now, Larkin. You're a lawman once again and you'd better start acting like one."

Thad knew the locals would be surprised to see a pastor wearing a badge. Best to get the explanations over with; the sheriff left the office to do his first round.

Larkin didn't get far before a group of townspeople circled him with questions. Thad revealed that he had packed a star years before and he hoped to return to being a full time pastor again soon. How soon? Well . . .

A scream which Larkin immediately recognized as coming from Maddie Johnson shrilled over the surrounding voices. Thad felt almost relieved as he shouted "Gotta go!" and broke from the circle.

Angry bellows followed Maddie's scream and all the noise was taking place near Sally's Dress Shop. Thad smirked: he usually thought of a ladies dress shop as being a quiet, civilized place. Maybe he needed to rethink that notion.

As he approached the store, Larkin spotted one of Maddie's twin cousins, he couldn't tell which one, standing in front of Sally's holding a pistol pointed at four people who were clumped together in the street immediately off the board-walk.

Larkin slowed his steps as he drew nearer to the store. The man with the gun was obviously nervous and angry. Thad didn't want to provoke him. The lawman could now hear the words which the gunman yelled.

"Maddie, you git back here with me, woman; do what I say!"

The lawman could now make out the four people facing the man in front of the store. There was Maddie, the center of the gunman's attention. Rebecca Torveen and Brad Myers formed bookends around her. Standing on the other side of the ranch foreman was Maddie's other cousin.

It was that other cousin who replied to the gunman's demand. "Maddie ain't goin' with you, Reuben. Miss Rebecca has invited her to go live with them and that's what she's gonna do."

"Shut your fool mouth, Ott," Reuben pointed his pistol directly at his twin brother. "Makes no never mind to me if we's kin. I ain't lettin' Maddie near Brad Myers. That snake is pleasurin' himself enough with Rebecca Torveen."

"You no good—" Myers lurched toward the gunman.

Ott grabbed Brad Myers by the arm and gestured for him to calm down. Myers took the advice.

With a casualness he hoped didn't look fake, Larkin stepped onto the boardwalk and ambled toward Reuben. As he did, the lawman noted that several people were watching at the window of the general store which neighbored the dress shop and a clot of barflies stared over the batwings of the Rome Saloon from across the street.

Plenty of people enjoying the misery of others but nobody lifting a finger to help: *Some things never change,* Larkin thought.

But the expression on the sheriff's face was kindly. "Good afternoon, Reuben."

"Go away, Preacher. I'm headin' for Hell and plenty happy 'bout it."

"Haven't you heard, Reuben, I have a new job."

"Huh?"

Thad pointed at the badge on his shirt. Reuben gawked in surprise. Larkin surprised him even more by knocking the gun out of his hand and quickly scooping it up.

Reuben made a fist and took a step toward the lawman. Larkin kicked his adversary on the ankle and sent him sprawling onto the boardwalk. Reuben shouted a curse at the sheriff as he returned to his feet.

Reuben Burke was preparing to take a swing at Larkin when his brother clamped an arm across his chest. "Let me go, Ott, you got no right to—"

"Calm down and stop actin' crazy. The sheriff's holdin' your gun and you already got yourself in trouble enough."

Reuben stared at the pistol in Larkin's hand. His eyes maintained a ferocious intensity but the rest of his body went limp with resignation.

There was a brief moment of silence which Thad broke with a question. "What exactly happened here?"

Ott Burke remained beside his brother, ready to stop any trouble. The three people left standing in the road glanced at each other as if trying to discern who would answer the question. Brad Myers took the job. "After Wes's funeral, Rebecca invited Maddie to come live at the Torveen ranch. They planned to meet here at Sally's—"

Rebecca interrupted her foreman, apparently

concerned he would say something that would embarrass Maddie. "Maddie and I plan to do a bit of shopping together before we head to the ranch. Brad needs to buy some things for the ranch from the general store."

"How does Reuben fit in?" Larkin asked.

"My brother don't fit at all or he shouldn't have," Ott spoke with a controlled anger. "When Maddie told us she's movin' in with the Torveens, Reuben got all ferocious-like. When he rode into town today, I knowed he had trouble in mind, so I followed behind him."

Larkin nodded his head before speaking. "Reuben, I'm arresting you—"

"No!" Maddie hurried onto the boardwalk. "Please, Reverend Larkin, let him go home. He didn't really intend to hurt nobody."

The sheriff glanced at Rebecca who nodded her head in agreement. Brad Myers shrugged his shoulders.

"OK, Reuben, but I don't want to see your face in town for six weeks, stay—"

Maddie once again interrupted. "Can't he come to church?"

Larkin inhaled deeply before speaking. For a moment, he felt more anger toward Maddie than he did toward Reuben. He inwardly laughed at his emotions and realized being both a pastor and a sheriff was going to create conflicts. "You can come into town on Sundays, Reuben, but only on

Sundays, for the next six weeks. Ride out. Now!"

Ott's voice was almost a whisper. "You're gettin' a lucky break, Brother, take it."

Without speaking, Reuben took the gun Larkin returned to him and stomped angrily down the boardwalk. Ott's voice remained low. "His horse is tied up near the Shootin' Star. I'll make certain he gets on it."

"Thanks, I appreciate it," Larkin said.

With the Burke brothers gone, Rebecca hurried onto the boardwalk and gently placed a hand on Maddie's arm as she looked through the store window. "Sally looks scared, let's go in and talk with her."

"Will talking with her make her not be scared?" Maddie sounded confused.

"I'm sure it will," Rebecca replied cheerfully. "And we need to do some shopping."

Maddie said nothing, her eyes focused on the store window where the gingham dress had once been displayed. Rebecca placed an arm around Maddie's shoulders and guided her into the shop.

Thad stepped off the boardwalk and exchanged whimsical grins with Brad Myers. The ranch foreman spoke as he watched the two women through the store's window. "Rebecca knew Maddie would have her some trouble going into Sally's. But the girl don't have much in the way of clothes. Rebecca didn't want her to feel bad 'bout that. She's buying her some things."

"That's kind of her, and kindness is what Maddie needs right now." Thad glanced into the store and saw Maddie Johnson smiling; it looked good on her. The lawman returned his eyes to Brad Myers. "What made Rebecca decide to invite Maddie to live at the ranch?"

Myers took off his hat and wiped his brow. "The Burkes are good folks and they tried to do right by Maddie, but she never felt like she belonged there, not even when she and Rebecca was friends back in school. When she started with all this talk 'bout being a witch the Burkes got spooked, jus' didn't know what to do."

"When did Maddie begin calling herself a witch?"

"Oh . . . round a year . . . a year and a half ago." Brad returned the hat to his head. "At first, folks jus' laughed at her but no more, lots of people think she has special powers."

"How about you, Brad?"

The foreman looked downward and toed the ground. "I don't know. I jus' don't know."

Chapter Fourteen

Brad Myers entered the general store and Thad could see that the ladies in the shop appeared to be busy and reasonably calm. He continued his round, much of which consisted of telling people that yes he was the acting sheriff of Creekside, Arizona. He had to tangle briefly with a couple of drunks at the Shooting Star who thought a pastor could be easily pushed around. *Might as well get used to that,* Larkin thought.

When he returned to the sheriff's office, he found Ott Burke standing in front of it. "Jus' wanted you to know that brother of mine is on his way home. I think he'll stay there for a while."

"Thanks, Ott." Thad took a key from his pocket and began to open the door to the office.

Burke waved his hand at the open doorway. "If you don't mind I got things to tell, things you need to hear."

"Sure, come in."

The two men entered the office; Larkin walked to the small pot bellied stove and the coffee pot on top of it. "The Lord saw fit not to bless me with the skill of making good coffee, but if you're willing to take a chance . . ."

"Sure, Preacher, I mean Sheriff, some java would taste good right now."

Larkin figured the young man wanted something to do while he talked and so didn't bother offering him a chair. Ott Burke was too restless to sit down.

Both men fussed with their coffee for a few minutes, then Ott blurted out, "There's somethin' not right about Maddie."

"Yes, Maddie is different."

"Why does God make some people like that?"

"I don't know."

"Maddie is plenty good to look at and that's gettin' her in trouble, a lot of trouble."

"What do you mean?"

Ott stared into his tin coffee cup as if summoning up the courage to continue. "Reuben has bad intentions when it comes to Maddie. It started . . . oh . . . less than a year ago, I guess. He started in talkin' about he and Maddie bein' kissin' cousins. My brother had a lot more in mind when it came to Maddie than jus' kissin'."

"Did Reuben ever try to force himself on Maddie?"

Ott nodded his head. "Not at the house, not with Pa around. But Maddie takes her fool rides into the woods, now and agin'. She's always liked to do that, ever since she could ride a horse. But lately she jaws 'bout goin' to get what she calls her special powers. She rode off late one afternoon, a few days back. Reuben waited a spell and followed after her. I did the same thing with Reuben. Mighty glad I did."

"What happened?"

"Maddie stopped by a creek to let her horse drink. My brother pulled up, dismounted and had just finished tyin' up his horse when I caught up with him. The fool was so excited he didn't bother lookin' back. He started peekin' through the tree branches at the girl. He was gettin' ready to . . . attack her. He'll say different but I'm sure that's what he was gonna do."

"And you stopped him."

"Yep, and Reuben didn't like it one bit. He threw a punch at me and I threw two or three back. My brother talks tough and fights like a little kid."

"How did Maddie respond to all of this?"

"She was upset plenty. But I don't think she knew what Reuben had in mind. She thought he was tryin' to find out where her special magic place was."

"Thanks for telling me all this, Ott. I'll pass it on to Rebecca, Brad and Owen. They need to know, not that they have any immediate plans for inviting your brother over for dinner."

Thad looked down for a moment and sloshed his coffee about in the dented cup. The lawman then changed the subject. "What do you know about Maddie's special powers, Ott?"

"Not much."

"What about the magic box Wes made for her?"

Ott made a dismissive laugh. "Maddie kept that thing hidden in the barn. I found it accidental-like, months ago. After takin' a look I put it back. There's nothin' to it."

"What do you mean?"

"It's jus' a wooden box with a little lever on the right hand side near the bottom." Ott raised a thumb and finger into the air and playfully twirled them about. "Turn that lever and the bottom board in the box will flip around."

"There's nothing more to it?"

"Pretty much. The bottom board has two holes in it big enough to run a string or wire through."

Thad ran a hand over his head as if trying to shake loose thoughts. "So, Maddie could tie something on the bottom of the box. By holding the box close to her and doing some hocus pocus to distract people she could turn the lever and make it look like something had magically appeared in the box."

"Reckon that's right."

"Do you know what all she made appear in the box?"

"Money. Maddie gives money to folks who needs it. She asked them to keep quiet 'bout it, but some people jus' can't keep their mouths shut. I tried to protect her, but couldn't always. One jasper took a big advantage of Maddie."

Larkin asked a question he knew the answer to, "Who?"

"Dean Ochs. That worthless drunk tole Maddie he had a sick little sister who needed to go East for an operation. You did ever one a favor by killing that lyin' rummy."

Ott's blunt statement hit Larkin in an odd way. Thad realized that, as a pastor, he should gently correct Ott for his harshness. But as a sheriff he had no such obligation. Larkin felt glad not to have the obligation and was a bit upset with himself for feeling that way.

"Thanks for the coffee, Sheriff." Ott placed his cup on the corner of the desk. "Guess I better get home. Not much lookin' forward to it. That brother of mine is gonna be plenty ornery."

"Can your family run the ranch without you, Ott?"

"Sure can. Fact is, I've been thinkin' about a job in town. I can read, ain't had schoolin' but—"

"How'd you like to be my deputy? The pay is twenty-five dollars a month and you get to sleep on a cot here in the office."

"Sure! After herdin' cows I'd plum enjoy herdin' drunks and fools."

"There's more to it than that."

"Oh, what else we gotta do?" The question was accompanied by a laugh. Ott Burke was happy with the job offer and his demeanor was becoming giddy.

"We need to find out who really killed Stanley Wiggins and Rob Laverty and we have to prove that Maddie didn't conjure up the ghost of Wes Torveen to walk the streets of Creekside and commit vengeance killings."

Ott's giddiness vanished. "Jus' how are we gonna do that?"

"That magic place in the woods Maddie always talks about." Thad paused, looked out the window, then looked back at his deputy. "If we can find that place, I think we'll find a lot of answers."

Chapter Fifteen

Rebecca admired the way Maddie Johnson handled the large knife. She sliced the bread roll perfectly. Rebecca also admired the fact that, unlike her, a night of little sleep didn't seem to bother Maddie. "Rebecca, do you think Louise will be upset to see me?"

Rebecca Torveen managed a kind, though artificial smile as she wrapped a hot pie in a towel. "Louise will be happy to see you, what made you ask such a question?"

The two women were working at the counter in the kitchen of the Torveens' ranch. They had already cleaned up after breakfast. "Louise has to be sad about losing her son, Josh. And, Wes was the man who killed him. He shouldn't have done that, but Wes changed, I'll tell Louise about it."

"Don't talk to Louise about Wes." Rebecca inhaled a ragged breath. She was tired and her nerves were brittle. "All you have to do is tell Louise you are sorry for her loss. She will be happy to have company."

"You visit her all the time."

"Not really." Rebecca placed the pie in a long box. "For the last year or so, ever since she has been in a wheelchair, Doctor Stamford has ridden out to see Louise once a month. I go with him and take along some baked goods."

"The Franklins are rich. Josh Franklin always dressed like a king. Why do they need charity?"

"Louise doesn't need charity, Maddie, she needs kindness. She needs to know that even though she is elderly and crippled and now dependent on her younger son to run the ranch, we still care about her and respect her."

"You're right and that's a wonderful thing to do. Thanks for letting me come with you." Something special came into Maddie's eyes as if she were gazing on her first Christmas tree.

Rebecca's nerves calmed. Maddie Johnson had loved Wes Torveen and Wes would be pleased to know that his family was providing Maddie with a good home for as long as she needed one.

Owen entered the kitchen and spoke to his sister in mock outrage. "You've made poor Maddie work on just a few hours of sleep and she doesn't get to eat any of the goodies! That's not fair!"

Owen's statement alarmed Maddie. "No, Mr. Torveen, Rebecca also got up early—"

"He's only joking," Rebecca cut in. "And call him Owen." She turned to her brother. "I thought you were going to repair a fence somewhere today."

"I am."

"Then stop eyeing food that's for the Franklins and get to work!"

Owen grimaced in a comical manner, and left

the kitchen with his head hung low. Maddie giggled and Rebecca's spirits were completely revived. Her brother had shown some reluctance when she suggested Maddie come to live with them. Rebecca couldn't blame him. Were those spells Maddie cast on Owen real or some strange form of mind manipulation? Rebecca didn't know but she was happy that Owen was trying to make Maddie feel at home on the Torveen ranch.

The kitchen door opened again and Brad Myers stuck his head in. "The doctor is here."

Rebecca quickly scanned the kitchen counter. Maddie was placing the sliced bread in the box beside two pies and a dozen doughnuts. "Tell him we will only be a minute."

"OK." The ramrod gave a wide salute and made sure his eyes took in both women. "Got a lot to do, I'll see you ladies later."

Both women replied with similar words. Brad closed the door partially shut and then gave Rebecca a quick wink. She winked back.

Fenton Stamford was pleased to see the two young women chatting together on the seat of the buckboard as they rode to the Franklin spread. The four horses in front of the wagon had made this trip often and needed little coaxing from Rebecca, who could make happy conversation with Maddie. The doctor reckoned there had been little to be happy about of late.

He rode on his black, a few steps behind the wagon. His horse also knew this ride well and Stamford's mind began to review the strange events which had ravaged the town of Creekside. There had to be . . .

A shot ricocheted off a nearby rock, shattering the doctor's private musings. Maddie screamed and the two lead horses reared onto their hind legs. Rebecca quickly gained iron control of the animals, and then prodded them to run at a fast but controlled pace.

Stamford spurred his black to where he was riding directly between the women and the rocky hill from which the shot had come. A second shot whined over the doctor's head. Fenton pulled his Colt from its holster and returned fire.

Fenton glanced toward Rebecca and nodded as she pointed toward a large boulder that protruded up ahead a few feet back from the road.

"Hold on tight, Maddie!" Rebecca pulled on the reins and the buckboard took a hard bounce as it left the road and hit the stony ground beside it. Maddie clutched the spring seat tightly as Rebecca guided the horses to pull the wagon behind the boulder.

"Keep down!" Rebecca shouted to her companion as both women jumped from the buckboard and scurried behind the large rock.

Fenton had dropped behind the wagon when it left the road, again trying to shield the women from any bullets. He hastily dismounted and tied his nervous black to the back of the buckboard. The mayor grabbed the Henry from the scabbard of his saddle and joined the two women behind the boulder.

Another shot came from the hill on the opposite side of the road from the boulder. The bullet whistled harmlessly into the blue sky.

Playful laughter sounded from the top of the hill. Stamford looked at Rebecca who stood directly beside him. "Whoever is up there on that hill seems to be having fun."

Rebecca squinted as she looked in the direction of the shooter. "He's firing at us but doesn't want to hit us."

Maddie who was on Rebecca's other side looked scared but no longer panicked. "Why would he shoot at us if he doesn't want to hit us?"

The question was quickly answered by a shout that roared from across the road almost as loudly as the gunfire. "Maddie, don't go near the Franklin ranch. I love yuh! Always will!"

"That's Wes! He's come back!" Maddie ran toward the hill. The action stunned her companions but only for a moment. Rebecca was the first to catch up with the frantic young woman, grabbing her arm before she reached the road.

"Maddie, get back behind the rock. We don't know—"

"I've got to go to him . . . Wes!"

Stamford latched on to Maddie's other arm. The doctor and Rebecca managed to half drag and half carry Maddie back to the boulder as the sound of hoof beats came from the hill.

"Don't leave, Wes . . . please don't leave."

Rebecca began to speak calmly to Maddie, the moment they had her back behind the boulder. "That wasn't Wes. Someone is playing a very cruel trick on us."

"Why would anyone do that?!"

"I don't know," Rebecca answered.

"Wes, please come back, please come back!"

Rebecca embraced Maddie as she gave in to tears. Fenton spoke softly to Rebecca as he pointed to his Henry which now lay propped against the boulder. "Use that if you need it. I'm taking a look at the hill."

Rebecca also spoke in a whisper. "Be careful."

Stamford once again drew his Colt as he ran across the road and began to ascend the hill. He didn't holster the gun but became increasingly convinced he didn't need it. Whoever had been shooting at them had ridden off.

At the top of the hill, his notion was confirmed. No one was there but that didn't make Creekside's Mayor one bit happy. The shooter had left behind a remembrance: a piece of gingham cloth ripped from the dress purchased by Wes Torveen.

Chapter Sixteen

Fenton Stamford paced about the sheriff's office as he spoke. "We need to keep this quiet for as long as we can. People are concocting enough superstitious nonsense as it is. We don't need stories about Wes Torveen coming back from the dead to warn Maddie not to go to the Franklin ranch. Louise Franklin is frail . . . she doesn't need to be dragged into all this!"

Thad Larkin looked at the piece of gingham cloth which now lay on his desk. Ott Burke stood beside the sheriff.

"What did you do after finding the cloth?" Thad asked the doctor.

"I put the cloth in my pocket and didn't mention it to the ladies. Rebecca could handle it, of course, but not Maddie. The ground around that area is hard and rocky and I'm not much good at tracking, didn't even try. I accompanied the women back to the Torveen spread, then came right here."

"You didn't go to the Franklin place?"

"No. It was just a routine visit. I'll go tomorrow . . . by myself."

"How's Maddie doin'?" the new deputy asked.

"Hard to say; she believes Wes spoke to her

today. She won't be going to the Franklin place, that's a sure bet."

Thad gave the piece of cloth a careful inspection. "Strange."

"There's plenty that's strange, all right," Ott said.

Larkin gave his two companions a chagrined look. "On the day of Wes's funeral, when I was still a pastor, Owen told me that the gingham dress had just disappeared. He saw Wes place it under the seat of the buckboard, and went to retrieve it that night but it was gone."

Ott shrugged his shoulders. "A lot of terrible stuff happened that day; wouldn't have been hard for someone to steal the dress."

Larkin picked up the cloth in what was almost an angry gesture. "Doctor, could you leave for the Franklin place early tomorrow morning?"

"Sure, but why?"

"Because I'm going with you. Ott, mind the store. Right now, I'm paying a visit on a banker."

The bank president caressed his desk as if it were a beloved pet. "I hope I have been of some help to you, Reverend Larkin, I mean Sheriff Larkin. Guess I'll take a while to get used to your new office."

"You've been a great help, Mr. Hawkins, and please just call me Thad."

Both men laughed good naturedly as they

stood up. "Fine, if you will start calling me Jim."

Jim Hawkins was the president of Creekside's one bank. He was an unpretentious man who appeared to be somewhere in his fifties. Indicative of his personality was the fact that he did not have a separate office. But, his desk did perch far enough away from the tellers cages to make a private conversation possible.

The front door of the bank almost seemed to explode open as a short, thin man stumbled inside. He was panting as he made his way toward Jim Hawkins. "Sir, there's something you need—Sheriff—good thing you're here!"

"Take it easy, Cliff, what is it?" Hawkins asked.

"Well, I was just walking by the Rome Saloon, now I didn't go inside, no, Sir, but the Rome is just a few doors away from the lawyer's office where you wanted me to take—"

"I'm sure you didn't go inside the saloon, Cliff." The bank president spoke calmly. "Now, what happened?"

"Murph Bohanan is in town! That man is a dangerous killer!"

Thad tried to match the calmness of Jim Hawkins. "Do you know what Murph Bohanan looks like?"

"No, but Horst Snider, the barkeep at the Rome, does. Horst was just getting to the Rome to start his shift when he saw Bohanan riding down the street on a big palomino. He called out to him to stop in at the Rome and have a free drink. Now, I saw all this happen, so I asked Horst if that was really Murph Bohanan. Know what he said?"

Hawkins gestured with his hand for Cliff to continue.

"Horst told me that the man surely was Murph Bohanan, he musta just rode in from Tombstone. And then he said, 'You and those other folks who work at the bank better watch yourselves,' that's what he said."

Larkin ran a hand over the back of his neck. "Horst was probably just shooting off his mouth. Bohanan is a gun for hire, not a bank robber."

Cliff's reply was swift and harsh. "How do you know? Bohanan coulda took part in bank robberies, a lot of innocent people get killed in robberies you know!"

"Thanks for bringing us the information, Cliff," Hawkins said. "You can get back to work now."

"I'm happy to be of help, Sir." Cliff gave the sheriff an accusing stare and then returned to his position behind the teller's cage.

Jim Hawkins shook his head. "Cliff is a good man, but he's easily excited."

Larkin's smile showed amusement. "Sheriffs and pastors have one big thing in common. Folks are always ready to tell you how to do your job."

"Looks like you've got a pretty tough job right now."

"Yes, guess I better get over to the Rome and welcome our town's newest visitor."

As he walked toward the Rome Saloon, Thad mused on how tough it was to know the truth about a gunfighter like Murph Bohanan. According to the dime novels, Bohanan had killed at least nine men.

I hope I don't get him into the double digits, Larkin thought.

Bohanan was easy to spot. Almost every eye in the Rome seemed to be on the gunfighter as he stood in front of the bar and finished telling a smutty joke to the customers.

As laughter screeched across the saloon, Bohanan gave everyone a quick wave and began to depart. Horst Snider motioned him back.

"Mr. Bohanan, you haven't even finished your drink!" A gleeful look suddenly filled the barkeep's face. "And lookee here, our new sheriff just come in. I'm sure he wants to meet you. Probably wants you to show him how to use a gun."

Another round of laughter filled the saloon. Laughter tinged with expectation and excitement. Maybe they would get to see Murph Bohanan in action.

The gunfighter strolled slowly back to the bar and picked up his drink. "Apologize for my bad manners, Horst." He looked directly at one of the saloon girls sitting at a nearby table. "If I come back later on, maybe ya can arrange some other free stuff for me."

The saloon girl raised her eyebrows and pursed her lips in a playful manner. Thad Larkin leaned against the bar only a few feet from the gunfighter.

"Murph, my name is Larkin. Like Horst told you, I'm Creekside's new sheriff."

"Well, please ta meet ya. Hope you're a good lawdog like Rob Laverty was. Yep, Rob was a sheriff who knew when ta leave a man alone."

The gunfighter's voice held a note of threat but didn't hold it well. A trace of nervousness ran through Bohanan's voice and body.

Thad quickly assessed the gunfighter. Murph Bohanan stood at slightly under six feet. Carrot colored hair topped a drawn, pale face. Baggy clothes testified to a man who had recently lost weight.

A lot of details didn't add up. Bohanan had appeared anxious to leave the saloon. He had started to leave without even finishing his free drink. The gunfighter seemed to have come in only because Horst Snider had called to him to do so. And the gun for hire had let it pass when Thad called him "Murph" instead of "Mr. Bohanan."

"How long are you going to be in town, Murph?" Larkin asked.

"Don't see how that's any of your business."

"How long are you going to be in town, Murph?" Larkin repeated.

Bohanan smiled and looked around the saloon, as if announcing that he had decided to toy with the sheriff. "Since yer so interested, I plan ta be here a spell."

"How long?"

A tic began to dance at the corner of the gunfighter's mouth. "I got me some business here in Creekside and plan ta stay 'til it's done."

As he finished speaking, Bohanan began to rub his arms and chest. Thad decided on a question most people in the Rome found strange.

"Are you a man who enjoys a pipe?"

A tinkle of laughter skittered around the saloon. Bohanan shrugged his shoulders before answering. "Yep. Some jaspers roll a smoke, others light a stogie. Me, I Iike a pipe."

Larkin's voice was a low monotone. "That's not what I mean and you know it."

"Don't folla."

"I don't think you'll like Creekside, Murph. We're not a modern town like Tombstone, no opium dens here."

"Ya got some mighty fool notions."

"If you don't like my notions, you're really not going to like Creekside. You see, this town has some very tough laws against the use of opium." Thad was lying. He didn't know what the local

123

laws said about opium and suspected they said nothing at all.

But Murph Bohanan bought it. "That don't make no never mind to me. I ain't never used that stuff."

"Well, that's good to hear, Murph. Now, if the saddle bags on that palomino of yours contained some illegal stuff, why, I'd have to confiscate it and put you in jail. But, I'm sure that's not the case. So I'll just have a quick look."

Larkin turned away from the bar, took one small step toward the batwings, then quickly pivoted and advanced on Bohanan who was going for his gun. The gunfighter barely had his .45 out of the holster when Larkin's fist smashed into his left eye. The gun made a rattling sound as it hit the floor. Murph Bohanan made a thump as he landed beside it.

The sheriff scooped up the gun and yelled, "Hope I didn't hurt your hophead too much, Murph."

Laughter once again exploded in the saloon but Thad Larkin didn't join in. The humiliation on Bohanan's face momentarily froze the lawman: it was a look of brokenness which could never be fixed.

Larkin still had a job to do. He grabbed the gunfighter by the arm and jerked him out of the Rome like a schoolmarm taking a bad boy out of class for a whipping.

Ott Burke came running down the boardwalk as Thad stepped out of the saloon with the gunman and let go of his arm. "Mr. Hawkins found me while I was doin' a round," Ott said. "Told me 'bout—"

A loud voice sounded from inside the Rome. "The sheriff punched Murph right in the eye. That hophead is gonna have a big grape on it!"

The gunfighter looked down and placed both hands over his ears trying to muffle the raucous laughter that once again blared from the Rome: laughter that was now aimed at him.

Thad eyed the hitch rail in front of the Rome and the fine palomino that was tied up there. Murph would be able to get a good price for the horse. For some reason, that notion brought Thad Larkin some comfort.

Bohanan walked toward his horse. The sheriff followed immediately behind him, rodding the bullets in the gunfighter's pistol onto the ground.

"This belongs to you, Murph." Larkin handed the gunman his empty weapon. Bohanan holstered it, and began to untie his horse.

"I don't want to see you in this town again, Murph." The lawman spoke in a firm voice which he then lightened a bit. "Go far away from here, change your name, give up the gun, and give up the opium—start over!"

Bohanan's voice was sharp and bitter. "Ya think yer so high and mighty, I—"

Four barflies barged out of the Rome Saloon and began to shout at the gunman:

"Hey, Murph, are you gunnin' after Wyatt Earp?"

"Go back to Tombstone and find yourself an opium den. Bet yo're king of the world in those places!"

"Shut up!"

Larkin's shout stunned all four men. One of them shouted back, "Sheriff, you got no call—"

Thad cut him off. "None of you have any business here. Move on or go back into the saloon."

Thad and Ott Burke were not surprised when the barflies returned to the saloon. Murph Bohanan had watched the louts with intense, fearful eyes as if he were watching his future.

Bohanan tried to speak again to the sheriff but his face began to contort. He pressed his lips together, mounted his palomino and rode out of town.

Larkin and his deputy stood in the street watching as Murph Bohanan became a dark speck in the vast sunlight. "You handled that good, Thad. You rid this town of a dangerous gunman without firing a shot."

"I'm not so sure."

"Whaddya mean?"

"A man like Murph Bohanan lives on his reputation. That's all he's got. Word gets around fast. Soon, he'll have nothing."

"Think he'll take your advice 'bout starting over?"

Larkin shook his head. "He'll retreat into opium."

Ott's eyes widened. "I just had me a thought. Once folks learn what's happened to Murph Bohanan, why, ever jasper around who wants to make a name will be bracin' him. Bohanan will be dead in a matter of months, sooner probably."

"Yes, and the only thing we can do for Murph Bohanan is pray for him."

"You may wear a badge now but you still talk like a preacher."

The two men returned in silence to the boardwalk and began to saunter back to their office. Ott Burke gave Thad a forced smile. "Well, at least we had ourselfs a little distraction from all these troubles about Maddie."

"Don't be so sure."

Ott raised his voice in surprise, "How can a gun for hire have any connection with Maddie?"

Thad took a key from his pocket and unlocked the door to the sheriff's office. "Bohanan said he had some business here in Creekside. I'm sure he was telling the truth about that."

The two men strolled into the office. "What kind of business do you reckon it was?"

"That's what we have to find out."

Chapter Seventeen

Ott Burke felt a mixture of strong emotions as he rode out to the Torveen ranch. The most powerful feeling was confusion. Ott believed he wanted to be a lawman but being the deputy to a sheriff who only two days ago had been a preacher . . . well . . . it seemed strange.

"Thad Larkin is a good man, but he ain't exactly what I had in mind regardin' a lawman," Ott said to his horse.

Burke patted his chestnut on the neck and continued the conversation. "Thad seemed right excited 'bout what he learned from the banker yesterday. Then, this afternoon he gets back from the Franklin place and tells me some of his notions."

Ott glanced upwards to where the sun's final glare splattered red over the mountains and hills. "Thing is, if a preacher says somethin' on Sunday mornin', he don't hafta prove it. If Thad Larkin's ideas is wrong now, well . . ."

The chestnut lifted its head and nickered. "OK, OK, I'll stop my complainin'."

Burke arrived at his destination and tied up his horse outside the Torveen ranch house. There were lights on inside and the sounds of people bustling about.

"Here goes," Ott gave his horse one more pat before walking up to the front door and knocking.

There was a slight pause in the bustle and the sound of a male voice shouting, "I'll get it!" Brad Myers opened the door.

"Well, well, if it ain't Creekside's new deputy; heard about you when I was in town."

"Yep, the preacher, I mean the sheriff, asked me—"

"Whaddya want?"

"I'd like to talk a spell with Maddie."

"She's helping Rebecca fix dinner. I would invite you to stay, Deputy, but I'm sure you have a lot of important duties back in Creekside."

"This won't take long."

"I said Maddie's busy, now—"

"What's going on here?" Owen Torveen appeared in the doorway.

Myers pointed a thumb at the lawman. "This jasper wants to see Maddie. He must think his brother ain't caused her enough trouble."

Owen Torveen smiled in a manner that conveyed a deep sadness. "You can't judge a man by his brother. I should know that better than anyone. Come in, Ott, I'll get Maddie. I'm sure Rebecca can spare her for a few minutes."

The deputy stepped inside. Brad Myers gave Burke a hostile stare and walked away. Ott felt sorry for the ramrod. Myers had tried to assume the role of the man of the house and had been stripped of his authority by the man who was really in charge. Ott had experienced similar humiliations in his life.

Owen returned with Maddie. There seemed to be no expression on the young woman's face and Ott couldn't tell how she felt about his sudden appearance. He tried to make some reassuring remarks about only needing to talk with her in private for a few minutes. Maddie nodded her head and left the ranch house with him.

"People say you're a deputy now," Maddie spoke as they stepped off the front porch.

"What people say is right."

"And Reverend Larkin is the sheriff?"

"He's only doin' it for a while, 'til things settle down."

The pair began to stroll toward a corral that stood in front of the ranch house on the far right side. The corral was four poled and contained two recently purchased horses.

"Is Reverend Larkin still going to preach on Sundays?" Maddie asked.

"Yep, he's plannin' on it."

"What if somebody tries to rob the bank or something during the Sunday service?"

"Guess that's why he's got me around."

Ott had intended his last remark to be at least modestly funny but Maddie didn't smile as they reached the corral. She leaned against the top pole and watched the two horses that frolicked

131

about, totally indifferent to their audience. The young woman then turned to the deputy as if expecting him to get to the point.

"Maddie, I know you've been through a lot lately, a whole lot. But I've got a favor to ask."

"You need money, don't you? People are only nice to me when they need money."

Ott Burke was stunned. In all the years he had known Maddie that was the first bitter statement he had ever heard from her. "It's not for me, it's for my ma and pa."

"Something wrong with the ranch?"

"Not exactly," Ott stammered. Lying didn't come easy to him. "Pa saw Doctor Stamford yesterday. Pa is very sick, medicine costs money and then there's a big hunk of cash they need to pay the bank next month."

The young woman continued to look at the horses, or maybe at something else that resided far beyond them. "Your parents were good to me. They didn't want me around, but they tried not to show it. I need to help them, but . . ."

Maddie went quiet and her silence made Ott increasingly nervous. "Have you lost your powers to do magic?" The deputy regretted the question the moment he asked it.

Maddie ran her fingers along the top pole of the corral as if she were drawing a picture in sand. "You know, the dress Wes bought for me disappeared."

"Yes."

"The magic box was a gift from Wes. It's all I have to remember him by. I don't want to use it for—"

She began to cry. Maddie didn't try to control her sobs or even to wipe the tears. Both of the woman's hands now grasped the top pole of the corral tightly as if she needed it to stop from collapsing. The deputy suddenly realized that, despite having practically grown up with her, he couldn't remember the last time he had seen Maddie cry.

Maybe crying will make her more normal. The lawman shook his head angrily as if trying to fling such a stupid thought from his mind. Ott then stood by silently for what seemed to him a long spell. Finally the woman pulled a handkerchief from a pocket in her dress. "I'm sorry."

"No cause to be."

"I don't want to use the magic box again. I don't want to be a witch, even a good witch anymore. But I should help Agatha and Dencel. I think God wants me to do that, don't you?"

"Ah . . . reckon."

"I'll ride over to their ranch soon." Maddie again went silent but this time she seemed to be doing some inward planning. "Would tomorrow be all right?"

"Sure."

"I should be getting back to the house now."

"I'll walk with you."

They walked in silence until they reached the front porch of the ranch house where the woman turned to face her companion. "Tell your ma and pa I'll see them tomorrow."

"I will, and thanks."

Maddie continued to talk as she stepped onto the front porch. "I hope this is the last time I'm a witch. Nobody loves witches except Wes Torveen and he's dead." She opened the front door, entered the house and vanished inside.

Chapter Eighteen

Ott Burke tensed up as he stood still as a stone on one side of the tool shed that fronted the Torveen Ranch. He listened to voices from behind the shed where he had been only moments before.

"Ain't nobody here! Are yuh satisfied now, Silas?"

"Reckon."

"Besides, anybody with sense woulda hid themselfs behind the barn where they got them plenty of cover."

"Reckon. But I coulda put my hand on the good book and swore I saw some jasper movin' back here."

"Come on, let's git us back to the bunkhouse. You're just jumpy because you're 'fraid of losin' ag'in at poker."

This time a chuckle accompanied Silas's, "Reckon." Ott listened carefully as the two ranch hands walked off, jabbering about cards.

Ott silently commended himself for being able to move around the shed and avoid the two loud and slow ranch hands who were investigating. But his commendation was cut short by the thought that he had allowed himself to be spotted. That couldn't happen again. There was too much at stake.

The deputy peeked around the side of the shed. His boss had been right. This location afforded him a good view of the ranch house, the corral which was on the right side of it and the large barn which stood about fifty yards from the front of the house and a little less than half that distance from the tool shed which was on its right.

His view of the bunkhouse which stood down from the corral was partially blocked by the barn. "Can't have ever thing," the deputy whispered to himself.

Thad Larkin had cautioned his deputy that patience was an important part of a lawman's job. "Guess I'm learnin' that early on," Ott's voice remained a whisper and he did not speak again for the next two hours plus, as he closely observed very little.

A hard sting on the back of his neck almost caused the deputy to give a yelp. But he stifled the impulse in his throat and turned to see his boss moving toward him. A small pebble hitting him from behind was a prearranged signal.

"How's it going?" Larkin asked.

Burke fought and defeated the temptation not to mention being spotted by a ranch hand. He thought it important to tell the sheriff everything. Besides, Thad Larkin would never lie to him. He needed to return the favor.

"I rode off from the ranch and tied up my

chestnut where you said. When I snuck back one of the hands spotted me but I hid and he got second thoughts. After that, I saw Maddie take the horses from the corral into the barn, then return to the house."

"Did she stay in the barn very long?"

"Now that you mention it, she was there longer than you might think."

Larkin nodded his head and, as both men had been doing, spoke in a whisper. "She could have been saddling her own horse, for a quick ride tonight."

Larkin's declaration about patience was once again put to the test. Another ninety minutes passed before Maddie Johnson left the house, now in complete darkness, and quietly moved toward the barn. She carefully opened the double doors, obviously not wanting to make any noise. Moments later she walked a saddled cayuse out of the large structure and, again moving with caution, closed the large wooden doors.

"Maddie loves that cayuse," Ott whispered in a sad tone. "Sometimes, she thought the horse was the only thing she really had. Know what I mean?"

Larkin nodded and remained quiet.

The young woman mounted and rode slowly around the barn staying as far from the bunkhouse as possible. Both lawmen pressed their bodies against the side of the tool shed, an unnecessary precaution. Maddie Johnson didn't look back as she rode off, quickening the pace of her cayuse.

"Good thing we got a bright moon and stars tonight," Ott's voice resounded with excitement. "Looks like Maddie is headin' for that special place in the woods she's always jawin' 'bout. Let's git our horses from that grove of trees back yonder and—"

Larkin hastily placed a finger on his lips to silence the deputy, then pointed toward the house where a figure was emerging from the front door. Whoever it was formed a shadow in the moonlight: a shadow whose identity was well hidden. The figure now stepping off the front porch wore a duster and a wide Stetson. Glancing toward the bunkhouse, the shadow seemed convinced that all the men there were asleep.

The figure ran behind the house and emerged on a saddled horse. The shadow then rode in the same direction as Maddie.

"What the—" Ott pushed his hat back and scratched the top of his head. "Do you reckon that jasper plans to hurt Maddie?"

"I don't think he intends to do her any good. Come on, we need to take your advice."

"My advice?"

"Get on our horses and follow," Larkin said.

Chapter Nineteen

The lawmen had no trouble picking up the trail of Maddie Johnson and her stalker. Trailing some-one at night is usually impossible. But the bright moon allowed Thad and Ott to pick up the tracks left by Maddie's cayuse and the horse of the person following her. Occasionally the lawmen could hear the rider in front of them. The stalker, not suspecting followers, wasn't listening for any. Still, Thad and Ott had to trail behind with caution.

Thad reckoned that the figure in front of them had taken the ride many times before as had Maddie. A theory of innocence exploited and criminal acts of desperation were beginning to take clear shape in his mind as the road became narrower.

Sounds of branches whipping about and horse-shoes clomping on stone caused the lawmen to halt their steeds. Several minutes later, identical sounds snapped in the night, this time causing a few small creatures to bolt to a safer location.

Larkin signaled to his deputy and the two of them veered off into the woods. They tied up their horses and pulled rifles from the scabbards of their saddles. Thad also removed field glasses from a saddle bag.

"We'll make our way through these woods," Larkin began to lead the way. "They provide a lot more cover than the road."

They came to a wide path which cut through the trees and shrubs. Branches from the trees arced over the path, making it appear almost ornate. Much of the ground was covered by large stones. Fresh dirt dotted those stones.

Thad turned to his companion. "This is where Maddie turned, along with whoever is following her."

"What do we do now?"

"Those tree branches provide plenty of darkness. Let's take a little walk and see what we can see." Larkin nodded at the weapon in Ott's hands. "Be ready with that Henry just in case we get spotted."

With Larkin again in the lead, the two lawmen made their way up the small slope on which the path ran. The sheriff made a halt sign, then employed his field glasses.

He saw a long clapboard structure whose sloppy workmanship made it look dilapidated even though the lumber was reasonably new. The hastily constructed building was circled by high bluffs, or almost circled. From what the lawman could spot from his location the bluffs parted behind the building. That gap probably led to a more travelled road which is why the jaspers involved in this operation usually employed the more obscure route used by Maddie. Still, Larkin reckoned that the back way led to a road going south to Mexico.

A great set up for a fast escape, Larkin thought.

A lantern hung over the front door of the cabin which did not have a porch. A man stood under that light talking to the figure the lawmen had been following, whose back was to Larkin. Maddie's cayuse was tethered to the ground. The young woman was nowhere in sight.

The figure on horseback rode to the back of the building and the man he had been talking to went inside. A few minutes later he emerged again this time following behind Maddie Johnson.

Maddie walked in an erect parade-like manner to her horse; her entire body seemed to ooze with anger. Thad listened carefully to the words she shouted at the man who was now busying himself with a cigarette.

"People who work for the government aren't supposed to act like you do. I'm writing a letter to the president!"

"You do that, girlie."

"Don't call me girlie!"

The man laughed and took a long drag on his smoke. Maddie stuffed something into one of her saddle bags, mounted and began to ride off.

The lawmen skedaddled back into the woods, and listened as the cayuse carried its owner away. Larkin crept back to the path, did a fast survey of the scene, then returned to his deputy.

"Whoever followed Maddie to this place is staying here," Thad said. "At least we know the woman is safe . . . for the time being."

"So, what next?"

"The fact that our friend in the duster is still here may mean that there are some big doings planned for tonight. We chose a fortunate time to get Maddie to visit her special place. We just got a lucky break."

Ott looked confused. "Jus' what do you plan on doin' with all this good luck?"

"Let's make our way up to the top of the bluff. That should give us a good view of whatever is happening tonight."

The lawmen were careful not to allow their feet to hit any hard stones or shake any gravel loose while they ascended the bluff. Reaching the top, they both lay flat down and observed the scene below.

"There are no horses tied up in front, which means they're all in the back," Larkin said. "So, there must be a back door to the building and probably a back window. That front window is big but they'd need another window in back for a half decent breeze."

"You think whoever bosses these jaspers cares all that much 'bout keepin' 'em comfortable?"

"Sort of, yes. The work they do isn't easy and, at this time of year, even the nights are hot.

Providing what fresh air is possible would seem a good idea."

Ott stared intently at the window of the cabin. "Looks like the jaspers inside are right busy. Are you still stuck on that notion of yours 'bout counterfeitin'?"

Thad also kept his eyes on the scene below using his field glasses. "Yes. Like I told you, after I killed Dean Ochs, Fenton told me to keep the hundred dollars Ochs had on him and use it for the church. That day, I locked the money in my office at the church and with everything going on, forgot about it."

"You forgot 'bout it, 'til yesterday, when you took it to Jim Hawkins, the banker."

Larkin continued to watch what he could through the cabin's window. There seemed to be three men inside, one of them busy with the chore of packing. The sheriff's excitement grew. The crooks could be readying the counterfeit money for a pick-up.

Thad took a deep breath, put the glasses down for a moment and replied to his deputy. "Jim Hawkins thinks the money is counterfeit but a very good counterfeit. He wouldn't have noticed it if I hadn't asked him to take a careful look. I also managed to pry some information out of him about Owen Torveen."

"What was that?"

"A couple of years back, Owen was way behind

with the bank. Then suddenly, he paid what he owed and hasn't been in any money problems since."

"You think Owen has been printin' his own money and payin' off his debts with it?"

"No," Larkin answered. "Owen is getting paid real money to make the phony stuff."

"Don't folla."

"I think Owen is working for some folks in Tombstone. The government has been coming down hard on counterfeiting. Tombstone would be an obvious place for a counterfeiting operation—too obvious. The counterfeiters needed to move their operation. Somehow, Rob Laverty got involved."

The deputy gave a low, caustic laugh. "Got no trouble believin' that, ever one knew Laverty was crooked."

"I think Laverty was the go between with the Tombstone people. Owen must have told him about his money problems and Laverty pounced." Thad again put the field glasses to his eyes. "Owen's ranch provided a perfect cover. There seems to be two men doing the actual counterfeiting. When they weren't working here they were posing as ranch hands at the Torveen spread."

"So, the folks in Creekside wouldn't be wonderin' about two jaspers that didn't seem to have much to do."

"Yes. I'm sure that was Owen riding ahead of us wearing the duster. He didn't want Maddie to know he was following her. Something important is happening tonight and he wanted Maddie gone."

"He musta heard me talkin' with Maddie. Guess I wasn't careful enough, sorry."

"Forget it," Larkin replied.

A few minutes of quiet followed as both lawmen continued to try and figure out exactly what was going on in the clumsy structure which the bluff almost circled. Ott broke the silence.

"How does Maddie fit in?"

Both men had been speaking in low voices but an element of sadness now crept in as Thad spoke. "Maddie likes to take rides by herself. She must have found this place at a time when Owen was here. Owen convinced her that this was a secret government operation . . . that Uncle Sam needed to be secret about where money was printed."

"That jasper probably fooled her into thinkin' he was a federal agent of some kind."

"And to make sure he kept her quiet he promised to give her some money now and then. Maddie took advantage of that promise to help people who needed money . . . or at least, people who could convince Maddie they needed cash."

Ott ran a hand over his forehead. "Why'd she

hafta go through all the witch stuff with the magic box?"

"We're always talking about Maddie being different. We forget she is also very kind. She knew how hard it would be for people to accept charity. But it wouldn't be so hard for desperate people to accept money produced by magic."

A quiver ran through Ott's voice. "You know I never thought 'bout Maddie bein' kind. I always jus' thought her loco. I feel kinda ashamed."

"I think we all underestimated Maddie."

"But what 'bout Laverty and Wiggins gettin' killed, how—"

Metallic screeches scorched through the night and both lawmen fell silent as a buckboard shot out from the trees which canopied the path and rattled toward the front of the cabin. The driver was wearing a red checkered shirt and Levi's that had a rope for a belt. His hat was wide and made of straw.

Larkin watched through his glasses as the man who had escorted Maddie out of the cabin once again appeared at the front door. He motioned for the new arrival to come inside and the driver quickly complied.

Thad began to chuckle as he kept the field glasses on the buckboard.

"What's so dern funny?" the deputy asked.

"Owen Torveen is a smart guy."

"Whattaya mean?"

Thad put the field glasses down. "Some owlhoots would have tried to move the money late at night."

"Isn't that what Owen's doin'?"

Thad pointed at the glasses lying in front of him. "That's what it looked like at first, but when our straw hatted friend walked into the cabin, they offered him some coffee. All the running about has stopped."

"Why?"

"The way I see it, they have packed most of the phony bills for transport, but they have also just completed one last run. They have to wait for those bills to dry."

"That'll take a couple hours."

Larkin chuckled again. "By the time straw hat hits the road, the sun will be coming up and folks who pass him by will see a man delivering flour."

"What?"

"There are four large sacks of flour on the bed of that buckboard that just pulled in. Those jaspers are putting counterfeit money in flour sacks and placing them under four actual sacks of flour."

"Jus' 'bout ever one needs flour. Folks would think they were lookin' at some harmless old coot deliverin' the stuff."

"Right," Thad replied. "And my guess is that the old coot isn't really old and isn't harmless.

There's probably a gun hidden under the bench of the wagon."

"Yep, and those four horses pullin' the thing look plenty strong. What are we gonna do now?"

"Well, Ott, our friends seem to be having a nice little social time, so let's pay a call on them."

Chapter Twenty

"I'll go down first," Larkin said, "and hide in those woods that run beside the back of the house. You follow behind me, and do the same only in the woods that run beside the front of the house. When you see me move over to the back window, do the same with the front window. When you hear me shout at those jaspers, let them know you have also dropped by."

Ott Burke replied with a quick, "Gotcha." Thad Larkin began to descend the bluff. As he moved downward carrying a Winchester, the sheriff began to experience an excitement he hadn't felt since he last wore a badge. He was closing in on a group of vicious thugs who had murdered and cheated decent citizens. Yes, he could get himself killed, but the lawman also knew what he was doing was worth it.

As he stepped into a row of trees, Thad wondered if this wasn't his true calling. Maybe becoming a pastor was a mistake, but then . . .

This is no time for meditation, Larkin thought.

The sheriff looked around a thick cottonwood to see his deputy follow his course down the bluff and into the woods. Behind the cabin stood a privy and another hastily built structure that served as a stable. Larkin smiled inwardly. The horses were far enough away that his arrival would not cause nervous nickering that could give him away.

Larkin stepped out from the trees, gave a wide, two fingered salute to his deputy, then advanced to the back window. He leaned against the side of the house and heard a voice he recognized as coming from Owen Torveen.

"You folks in Tombstone are supposed to be so damn smart, Finch. Why'd you send Murph Bohanan? Even a green sheriff, a preacher yet, spotted him as a hophead."

Both the front and back windows were located not much higher than Thad's waist. The shutters were wide open. The counterfeiters were obviously confident no one would find their location except Maddie and saw no good reason to camouflage their operation. The sheriff took a quick look inside and tried to assess the situation.

Owen Torveen had taken off his duster and Stetson. He was talking with the man in the checkered shirt and straw hat, who looked younger and stronger than his modest clothing would indicate from a distance. The two other men appeared to be the actual counterfeiters. One was heavy set and short; the other was tall and bald and was the man Thad had seen outside of the cabin. Both counterfeiters wore guns.

Torveen and straw hat were standing near one end of the long cabin which boasted a pot bellied stove and two cots. The counterfeiters were standing on the other end near the printing press where they performed their work. A table stood in the middle of the cabin and now held rows of counterfeit money in the process of drying.

Straw hat threw up his arms as he replied to Owen's complaint. "All right, all right, Murph was a good talker and he convinced us he could take Rob Laverty's place."

"How did you think he could do that?" Owen shouted. "Bohanan wasn't the sheriff, held no office at all and sure wasn't going to get one. He couldn't manipulate matters to keep the operation secret. Living in Tombstone doesn't make you smart, Finch. Hell, a mule is smarter than you."

After his first glance into the room, Larkin had pulled back and was now standing beside the window. But the lawman figured Finch couldn't let an insult pass. Thad again moved his eyes to the corner of the window.

The two counterfeiters were watching Finch intently as he took threatening steps toward Torveen. The ranch owner stood in place but leaned his body backwards and began to raise one arm as if preparing for an assault.

Finch pushed a finger into Owen's chest. "You're maybe forgetting a few things. Like, if it weren't fer us letting you in on our business deal, you woulda lost that precious ranch of yours way back."

Owen moved his arms about in motions of appeasement. "Look, Finch, I'm sorry—"

Finch pressed harder with his finger, forcing Torveen to stumble backwards toward the stove. "You oughta be sorry, Owen. You ain't so smart yourself." He pointed at the tall counterfeiter. "Harry tells me that crazy woman was here tonight."

"It was the last time. I promise."

"Oh, you promise." Finch barked a laugh. "Like that promise you made about getting rid of her. Dooley, did that idiot girl look dead to you?"

The short, pudgy counterfeiter gave an anxious smile. He seemed pleased to be let in on the conversation. "No, Finch she was alive plenty."

Finch kept his eyes on Torveen. "You heard what Harry and Dooley said, was they telling the truth?"

"Yes, but—"

"That girl is loco!" Now Finch was shouting. "Who knows what she might tell anybody! I want her dead!"

"I'll take care of it, I—" Owen started to say, "I promise" but thought better of it.

Finch took another step toward Torveen. The two men were barely an inch apart. "You better take care of it. You see, Owen, we're gonna find the right man to replace Rob Laverty and there's no reason we can't replace you."

Tension seemed to freeze the four men in the cabin. Larkin decided to move. "Hands up, every one of you! You're under arrest!"

Ott immediately appeared at the front window, pointing his Henry at the outlaws. "You heard the sheriff, we got you covered."

Owen Torveen and the two counterfeiters glanced quickly at the two windows. Their eyes then shifted to Finch who was raising his hands and they followed his example.

Panic laced Torveen's voice. "You got this wrong, Thad. I—"

"Shut your fool mouth," Finch's voice was a low rumble.

"Good advice," Larkin shouted through the open window. "Ott, take their guns."

Ott Burke cautiously entered the cabin through the front window. He disarmed Torveen first, taking the Smith and Wesson from Owen's shoulder holster and tossing it through the window. Keeping his Colt firmly in hand, Ott advanced to Finch and patted the outlaw down.

Satisfied that Finch wasn't carrying a weapon, Ott moved on to the counterfeiters, each of whom had a Colt strapped around his waist. Larkin's attention riveted on Finch, who, keeping both hands raised, casually moved his left arm over to tap his right wrist.

"Look out, Ott!" Larkin shouted as a derringer propelled into Finch's right hand.

Finch plunged to the floor, avoiding the shot from Larkin's Winchester by inches. Larkin levered his rifle and fired at Harry who had palmed his Colt. The outlaw spun, dropped his gun and began to stagger about the room. He collided with the table and went down with it. Stacks of counterfeit bills fell on his body.

Ott kicked the derringer out of Finch's hand and then turned toward Dooley a moment too late. Dooley slammed a foot into the backside of the deputy's knee and started to go for his gun as Ott went down.

"Freeze Dooley!" Larkin shouted from the window.

"Don't shoot," Dooley dropped the gun and raised his hands again. "I ain't no killer, not like Harry."

Thad gave the entire cabin a quick look. The front door stood open. Owen Torveen and Finch had vanished.

"You OK?" The sheriff asked his deputy through the window.

"Yep, sorry 'bout not checking Finch's wrists," Ott looked around quickly as he returned to his feet. "Guess that jasper got away."

The noise of a clanging buckboard silenced Ott. Larkin turned his head as four horses pulled the wagon past the cabin toward the back road. The sheriff gave his deputy a fast look.

"I'm fine here, go!" Ott yelled.

Larkin dropped his Winchester and ran after the buckboard. This time, the cleverness of the outlaws was working against Finch. They were using an old wagon to create the illusion of a harmless work buggy. The wagon squeaked loudly, covering the sounds of Larkin's pounding steps.

Thad's one chance to catch up to the rig came as the outlaw arrived at the area where the bluffs parted. Finch had to slow the buckboard to navigate the twist in the road. Finch pulled back on the reins and focused his eyes on the horses. The road leading south was tantalizingly close but it would require careful maneuvering to get there.

Thad grabbed the tailgate of the wagon and yanked himself on board, landing on one of the flour sacks which muffled the sounds of his body hitting the flatbed. Finch did not turn around, unaware of the intruder.

Larkin mused over his good luck as he brought his breathing down to a normal level. He drew the Colt which had partially slipped from his holster and made an awkward but fast crawl to where he could jam the gun's barrel into the back of Finch's neck.

The buckboard has just passed through the bluffs when Larkin ordered, "Stop this wagon, Mister. You're not going anywhere."

The outlaw was stunned but remembered what

Torveen had said: ". . . a green sheriff, a preacher yet . . ."

"Sure Sheriff, looks like you got me good. I give up, jus' need a moment to pull up these nags."

Finch yelled a theatrical "whoa!" at the horses as he raised his arms but did not pull up the reins. He tried to slam an elbow into Thad's head. Larkin did a half twist of his neck to avoid the attack as Finch began to reach under the bench where a rifle was stowed. Thad slammed his Colt against Finch's skull, sending his adversary tumbling to the ground.

Larkin moved onto the bench and grabbed the reins. He gained control of the horses and turned the buckboard around. As he drew near to Finch he slowed the animals and held the reins in one hand, freeing the other for his Colt.

He pulled up beside the outlaw. Did Finch have another small gun hidden on him? The lawman needed to resolve that question quickly. He jumped from the wagon and cautiously approached the outlaw.

Finch greeted Thad with a bellow of obscenities followed by, "My leg is broken."

Thad crouched beside the outlaw and inspected his clothes, finding another derringer lodged in a boot. He shook his head in mock outrage. "I guess it's true what folks say about Tombstone, nothing but a cesspool of sin housing the worst snakes that ever crawled the earth."

Larkin smiled as he tucked the small gun into his belt. Finch wasn't amused. "Damn you, my leg's broken, hurts awful."

The outlaw pointed at his right leg which lay at an awkward angle. *Impossible to fake that,* the lawman reckoned.

"Finch, I need to move you to a nice comfortable spot."

"Whattya talkin' 'bout?"

"You're going to be resting on a nice soft bed of flour sacks."

Larkin brought the buckboard to a stop behind the cabin. Ott Burke was stepping out from the small stable. Dooley was with him, his hands tied behind his back. Dooley gave no sign of contemplating escape. The deputy's six gun was in his holster.

The quizzical expression on Burke's face turned to glee as he stepped close enough to the wagon to see what was lying on the flatbed. "Looks like you got a passenger, Thad, or should I call him a prisoner?"

Finch shouted another string of obscenities as he vowed vengeance on the lawmen. Both the sheriff and his deputy noted the emptiness of the threat.

Dooley also realized Finch was heading for a long prison stretch or possibly a rope. "Look men, I jus' played a small part in all this. I made funny money, not claimin' different, but I never hurt nobody."

"Keep quiet, Dooley, if you know what's good fer you—"

"You're not the big man anymore, Charlie Finch!" Dooley's pleading eyes bounced between Thad and Ott. "I'm jus' an artist, couldn't make much of a livin' paintin' pictures."

Larkin smiled whimsically. "So, you decided to paint money."

"Some bad men took advantage of me," Dooley's words scrambled together. "And I know who they are, I mean the big bosses in Tombstone; I'll testify against them in court. All I ask is for a lenient sentence. Think you fellas can help me out?"

Larkin continued to smile. "Sure Dooley, you do what you just said, and I think we can manage to bring the judge to a more profound understanding of artistic license."

Dooley looked happy and so did Ott Burke. A few seconds of silence followed before Larkin asked a question for which he already knew the answer. "How's the other man, the one named Harry?"

"Dead," Ott replied. "I think he was gone before he hit the floor."

"Probably," Thad answered abruptly before changing the subject. "Seen anything of Owen

Torveen?"

" 'Fraid not." Burke pointed backwards with his thumb. "Jus' checked the stable. The horses there are unsaddled and haven't been rode for a spell. Way I see it, Owen ran when all of the shootin' was goin' on in the cabin. He got his nag outta the stable and right now is ridin' for the border."

"I'm sure you're right about most of it. You know, Ott, I almost hope he is riding for the border."

"I don't follow you."

"I have some notions I hope aren't true."

Larkin jumped off the buckboard and shifted the conversation. "I'm going to get our horses. I want you to take the two prisoners into town."

Ott looked at Dooley. "I think I can trust our artist friend to drive the wagon if I'm riding close by."

"Sure!" the counterfeiter said anxiously. "I'll do all I can to help the law."

Thad glanced at the flatbed. "Finch is passed out. You better get him to Doctor Stamford first thing."

"You're not ridin' with us?" The deputy asked.

"No, I can't. Those notions I was talking about, they just may be right."

Chapter Twenty-One

Maddie Johnson stared in awe at the large gates that towered over her. She had often heard them called the pearly gates. She had supposed that "pearly" meant made of pearls but these gates were shiny with the color of gold. Yes, they were made of pure gold!

Her feet felt as if she was walking on air and, that's exactly what she was doing. The clouds under her seemed to caress her ankles with a wonderful softness and warmth.

The gates slowly opened and a figure emerged. As the figure walked toward her, Maddie's awe became excitement: it was her mother! She looked even more beautiful than she did in the one picture Maddie had of her, a picture which had been taken when Maddie was a baby.

The woman ran to her daughter and embraced her. The two women held on tight to each other.

Maddie's mother slowly let her go and then stood back to admire her. "I'm so happy to see you."

"I'm happy to see you, Mother. Have you met Wes?"

"Yes, honey, he's here and he's such a wonderful man."

Maddie's excitement grew. "Let's go see him together, right now."

The young woman suddenly felt scared as a distressed look creased her mother's face. "I'm afraid that's impossible. You will never see Wes or me again."

"Why?"

"That was such an evil thing you did, pretending to be a witch. Fooling people into thinking you had magical powers. You can never enter Heaven."

"I'm sorry, Mother, I didn't mean for Stanley Wiggins and Rob Laverty to get killed. I just said those things at Wes's funeral because I wanted to scare them, punish them for . . ."

"Such an evil thing."

The voice of Maddie's mother became increasingly faint as she vanished in swirling clouds. Maddie Johnson was now alone as clouds circled her, blocking the woman's view of Heaven's gate. The clouds turned to smoke and she could see flames rising up. From a distance she could hear Wes's voice, "Maddie, Maddie . . ."

The woman opened her eyes. She was lying in her bed in the room she had been given at the Torveen ranch. Maddie thought back on the previous few hours. She had returned from her special place in the woods with the money for Agatha and Dencel, feeling very sad and very tired. She had taken off her boots and dropped onto the bed to relax for just a moment when . . .

"Maddie . . . Maddie . . ."

Wes's voice continued to call her from the dream. But she was awake now and the voice was accompanied by a tapping on the shutters of her bedside window.

Maddie left the bed and slowly approached the window. "Wes, is that you?"

"Yep, I've come for yuh, darlin'."

"I was just dreaming about you. We were in Heaven, kind of—"

"We're gonna be in Heaven together forever. Open the shutters, darlin'."

The young woman opened the shutters and placed a hand over her mouth to muffle a scream. Wes Torveen's face filled the window. In the background a black sky was gradually surrendering to gray.

Tears puddled at the corner of Maddie's eyes. "Wes, this is a miracle!"

"Yes, darlin', a miracle, but I ain't no ghost." He reached a hand through the window and caressed her cheek.

"You're real, Wes, flesh and blood."

"Sure am! Now git out here quick."

Maddie laughed uncontrollably as she put on her boots. She thanked God with a broken voice as she bolted from her room and ran down a hall to the house's living room and front door.

"Maddie, what's going on?!" This time the

voice was feminine and right behind her. Maddie stopped at the door and watched her friend approach as she silently admonished herself for not being quiet. Rebecca's room was next to hers.

Maddie leaned against the door, feeling confused. Rebecca seemed to be a herald of reality, a reality which didn't allow for Wes Torveen to return from the dead. And yet . . .

Rebecca tied the sash around her green robe, before grabbing Maddie by her shoulders. "What's happened?"

"Wes is back, he just talked to me, he's waiting outside."

"Maddie!"

"It's true, it's true!"

"OK, honey, we'll go out together and see Wes."

"I'm not sure he wants you there, Rebecca."

"I'm his little sister! Wes put up with me all his life. I don't think he'll mind seeing me now."

Rebecca's humourous response vanquished Maddie's anxiety. She giggled and spoke with a childlike excitement. "You're right! Let's go, he's waiting."

The two women ran outside. Rebecca followed Maddie as she made fast tracks to the side of the house.

Rebecca was shocked when she first saw the man standing beside the open bedroom window. It really was Wes! He was wearing the clothes he had been buried in: a suit with a black frock coat and a gold colored vest.

But wait . . . Rebecca took a closer look. The vest was actually a light yellow. Her older brother owned a yellow vest as well as a black frock coat.

"Wes!" Maddie embraced the man and buried her face into his shoulder. She began to cry as Wes coiled his left arm around her. Rebecca closed her eyes and clenched both of her fists for a moment, trying to keep her emotions in check. Yes, she wanted Wes to be alive but she also knew that was impossible.

As she opened her eyes she could see the man who called himself Wes staring directly at her. The early morning provided only scant light, but to Rebecca that stare looked hostile.

Maddie gradually broke away from Wes's embrace and employed both of her hands to wipe away tears. "I'm sorry but I wasn't expecting a miracle, I guess that makes me a bad person."

"No, Maddie, you're the finest lady I've ever known. But we gotta leave here. I already got horses saddled in the barn. Me and you are gonna be together forever."

"Aren't you going to even say hello to me, Wes?"

"Sure, Sis, sure, happy to see you and all." Rebecca noted a slight change in the man's voice and listened carefully as he added, "But Maddie and me can't stay. We need to be going."

Maddie smiled brightly; she was accepting this man's claims. Rebecca knew she'd have to handle this by herself. "OK, Wes, all I want is for you and Maddie to be happy."

"Thanks, Sis, now we gotta get goin'."

Rebecca figured it wasn't only her that was making the man jumpy. Soon, all of the ranch hands would be rising. The man standing in front of her knew that. "Just one more thing, Wes; I want to give you and Maddie a gift."

"You don't have to give us anything," Maddie exclaimed. Her face was flushed with joy. Rebecca felt almost guilty for what she had in mind.

"Remember just before you left Creekside, Wes, you made a magic box for Maddie and a small wooden cross for me?"

"I remember."

"I've worn that cross around my neck ever since." Rebecca took two steps toward the couple as she hastily lifted the ribbon which held the cross over her head and extended the hand that held it. "I want to return the cross to you."

"No need."

"I want you to have it!" Rebecca's voice was kindly as she moved closer to the couple. "That way you can give it as a special gift to Maddie. Here!"

Rebecca threw the small wooden object at the

man calling himself Wes. He reached out and caught it.

"Death looks good on you, Wes." Rebecca's voice became shrill with mockery.

"Jus' what are yuh jawin' 'bout, Sis?"

"You caught my toss with your right arm." The woman moved closer to her brother. "Why are you doing this, Owen? Why the fake beard, why—"

"I ain't him!" Owen threw the cross onto the ground. "Owen Torveen is dead. I killed him."

Maddie Johnson's joy morphed into confusion and terror. "Wes, you said you'd stop killing."

"I had to kill that man." Owen glanced at Maddie, then looked at his sister with eyes of hatred and loss. "Remember that time, when we was kids, when Josh Franklin invited Owen and me to his daddy's ranch?"

Rebecca cautiously moved closer to her brother. She was almost within arm's reach and could see that he had even placed a purple mark on his cheek. She was about to ask him how he had done it, before jerking herself back to reality. Owen was insane. She had to be careful. "Yes, I remember that time . . . Brother . . . what of it?"

"Josh Franklin tried to shoot me in the leg. He wanted me to have a crippled leg as well as a crippled arm."

"Owen told me about that," Maddie's voice quivered. "He went to get Josh's parents—"

"He was lyin'" Owen shouted. "Josh's folks were ridin' nearby and heard the shots. They came and stopped Josh before he put a bullet in me. Owen set me up for Josh to shoot me. Owen wanted so bad to be friends with the son of a rich man. He was ashamed of bein' poor and was willin' to get me shot jus' to be able to visit a rich man's ranch anytime he wanted."

Rebecca was beginning to have some inkling of the horrible demons that raged inside her brother. Acting on instinct she opened her arms and moved toward Owen to embrace him.

"Stay where you are!" Owen took a step backwards and drew his gun, using his left hand. "Yuh shouldn't have interfered, Rebecca. Maddie and me's got important plans for today and you're not stoppin' us. You're gonna do jus' what I'll say or I'll kill yuh."

"No, Wes, you promised—"

"Quiet, Maddie, yuh don't understand," Owen's voice carried a note of desperation as if he also didn't understand. "But you're gonna . . . real soon."

"I know you, Brother, you wouldn't kill me." But as Rebecca looked into Owen's eyes she realized her words were false. She no longer knew Owen Torveen and the man standing in front of her now was very capable of killing her.

Chapter Twenty-Two

Thad Larkin pulled up in front of the Torveen ranch house. He flipped his horse's reins around the hitch rail and ran onto the porch. The front door opened before he could knock on it.

"Morning, Preacher, paying an early visit?" Brad Myers spoke as he stepped onto the porch and closed the door behind him.

Larkin didn't have time to explain he was acting as a lawman. "Is Owen inside?"

Myers didn't catch the urgency in Thad's question. "Nobody's inside. Owen's probably makin' his way to the bunkhouse to talk with the hands. I need to check with him 'bout some things that need doin' today. Want to go over some stuff with the hands while they chow down on breakfast."

"How about Maddie and Rebecca?"

The foreman laughed and shook his head. "Rebecca keeps an eye on Maddie. Who knows where they're off to, I like Maddie but—"

"You're heading for the bunkhouse?"

Myers gave a slight shrug. "Yep."

"I'll check the barn."

"Sure." Concern crept into Myers's voice. He started to ask if anything was wrong but Thad was already making a run for the barn.

． ． ．

The double doors of the barn stood open and Larkin immediately spotted fresh tracks in the soft ground. He started to go into a crouch for a closer look at the dirt when muffled screams came from the back of the building.

The lawman bolted into darkness. There was not yet any sun to penetrate the open doors. He found Rebecca tied hand and foot with her mouth gagged. Thad untied her as quick as he could, noting that whoever had done this knew something about tying knots.

"Thank you, Pastor, thank you . . ." Rebecca shook her arms and legs for a few moments to restore circulation and then, with some help, got back on her feet as she brushed dirt out of her hair and off her robe.

"What happened?" Thad slowly removed his arms from the woman, confident that she was now able to stand without assistance.

Rebecca gave the sheriff a quick account of Owen's appearance as Wes. "Owen forced me to come to the stable with him and Maddie. Reverend, I think he would have killed me only a shot would have awakened the ranch hands."

"Did he ride off with Maddie?"

"Yes, Pastor, they . . . I'm sorry, I forgot you're the sheriff—"

"Never mind, do you know where they're going?"

"Yes, they're riding to the place where Wes and Maddie used to meet when they were school kids. I heard Owen tell Maddie they had to go there. Maddie told us about those meetings on the day we buried Wes. Strange thing . . ."

"Yes?"

"Well, like I said, Wes threw my wooden cross to the ground when I tricked him with it. But, before coming to the stable, he made sure Maddie picked the cross up and placed it around her neck. I can't understand why Owen is pretending to be Wes."

"Owen isn't pretending. I can't explain it right now, but Owen really believes he is Wes. Do you know where Maddie's magic box is?"

"Yes, she keeps it in her room."

"Does Maddie believe Owen when he says he's Wes?"

Rebecca nodded her head vigorously as her face reflected pain. "She wants so badly to believe it . . . yes."

"Get into some clothes quick, and grab the magic box, we have to ride after them."

"Should I tell Brad? He could come with us, maybe bring some of the hands."

"No, this isn't a job for a posse. Owen is holding the cards. He could hear a lot of horses coming. We have to handle this carefully."

"Do you think he'd hurt Maddie?"

"He's going to kill her, and then kill himself."

Chapter Twenty-Three

"This is my favorite time of the day," Maddie looked up at the sky now splattered with patches of red. "Can we stop and maybe just look for a moment . . . not too long?"

"Sure, darlin', I want yuh to be happy."

The couple reined up. The young woman stared at the sky. Her hands were shaking. She needed to control herself before Wes noticed her nervousness. But was the man now looking at her really Wes? Maddie believed miracles did happen but she also knew that Wes had never called her "darlin' " until today.

"Yuh look worried, darlin', what's wrong?"

"Oh, I'm just thinking about Rebecca. Wish you hadn't tied her up like that. I should have stopped you. Rebecca's always been nice to me. We weren't very nice to her this morning."

Wes gave a loud, exaggerated laugh. He had never laughed that way before. As he lifted his head, Maddie realized Rebecca was right. Wes's beard was phony and his purple birthmark didn't look right.

"My sister is out of those ropes right now." Wes suddenly paused and inhaled as if the thought of Rebecca being free made him uneasy. "Yuh know, the ranch hands are up and by now one of them has been to the barn and found Rebecca."

"When you tied her up, Wes, you used your right hand and you've been using your right hand while we ride."

"Yuh had enough starin' at the sky?"

"Yes."

"Then, let's git movin'."

Maddie's fear was escalated by Wes's gruff voice. She didn't look directly at her companion as they continued their ride but her face became pale white from the sharp emotions running through her.

"Darlin', there's somethin' I need to tell yuh 'bout myself."

"What's that?"

"Well, yuh know what it says in the good book 'bout how all of us has souls?"

"Rebecca and I have been reading the Bible together."

"The Lord has worked a real miracle in my case."

Wes's references to God and the Bible were easing the woman's fears. "What kind of miracle?"

"Yuh was right 'bout my right arm and all. Sounds kinda strange, I know, but the good Lord has brought my soul down from heaven and placed it in Owen's body."

Maddie was stunned. What she had just been told made some sense to her; it explained Wes's use of his right arm, but questions circled her like angry bees. "What happened to Owen's soul?"

"It's in Hell where it belongs."

The woman gasped and looked at her companion in disbelief. "That can't be, Owen is a good man!"

"You're wrong, Owen is a terrible man."

Wes's voice once again sounded different, more like Owen. Maddie's hands continued to shake as she suddenly turned and looked behind her. "We've passed it."

"What?"

"Our special place, we rode by it."

"You sure?"

"Yes." She leaned her head toward the creek. "This is the area where there's no large stones or even small ones."

"So?"

"Remember, our special place is where there's that big stone, the one you said looked like a dog sitting on its hind legs?"

"Ah . . . right. Guess we'd better go back."

The couple stopped and turned their horses around. On the ride back, Maddie watched her companion. He was eyeing the terrain in what seemed to be an effort to spot the sitting dog boulder.

"Guess we're here!" Wes proclaimed loudly but the woman caught the uncertainty in his voice.

"Yes," Maddie replied. They dismounted, tied up their horses in a cluster of trees and walked toward the sitting dog.

"I was tellin' yuh the truth." Wes spoke in a low gravelly voice and Maddie noticed that once again he sounded like Wes.

"You mean about Owen?"

"Yes."

"You need to learn forgiveness," Maddie paused for a moment. She felt odd telling a soul who had just returned from Heaven that he needed to learn forgiveness but she plowed on. "What Owen did to you back when you were boys was terrible, but it was a long time ago."

"That ain't all of it. Owen murdered me and that wasn't a long time ago."

"What!?"

They stopped in front of the sitting dog boulder. Wes stared at Maddie with something in his eyes that scared her.

"Owen conspired with Rob Laverty, Stanley Wiggins and Ed Horton to ambush me in front of the general store. Owen was the worst one of the whole damn bunch!"

"What do you mean?"

"Owen pretended to be protectin' me. Acted like he was riskin' his own life by jumpin' on the flatbed of the buckboard and helpin' me to shoot it out with Laverty and Wiggins after I brought down Ed Horton. The wonderful big brother! I'll tell yuh how damned wonderful he was, he ran over me with the buckboard. Now yuh know why his soul's in Hell!"

"I just can't believe—"

"Yuh gotta believe it, Maddie. Owen was a liar, a fraud, a selfish man who cared 'bout no one 'cept himself. And now he's burnin' in Hell for it!"

Tears cut loose from Maddie's eyes. "Wes, I want to go back home."

"We're both goin' home, Maddie. Right now, we're goin' home together."

"That's wonderful." Maddie embraced Wes and for a few minutes cried as he gently caressed her head.

She broke away from him and gave a whimsical laugh as she brushed away tears. "We'd better start back now. Rebecca will be worried."

"That's not what I meant when I said we was goin' home."

"What?"

"I can't stay here on earth. I'm goin' back to Heaven and you gotta come with me."

Maddie stepped back from Wes and asked a question she feared she knew the answer to, "How are we gonna do that?" Wes held out both arms as if getting ready to hold the woman in a tight grip. "It'll be painful for just a minute, and then it will be wonderful and we will be together forevermore!"

"You're going to kill me!" Maddie looked at the gun resting against Wes's left hip. "You're gonna shoot me dead!"

"It'll only be a brief moment of pain and then we'll be in Heaven."

"Wes wouldn't do anything like that to me. You're not Wes, you're Owen!"

Maddie turned and ran. Owen stood immobile for a moment. He started to draw his gun, but stopped. He couldn't kill Maddie from a distance. It had to be up close, and then he would immediately kill himself.

Owen ran after the woman. As he drew nearer he had to duck the stones Maddie threw at him. Picking up those stones slowed the woman and Owen was able to grab Maddie from behind and turn her around. Maddie tried to hit him with a rock she held in her right hand but Owen twisted her arm, forcing her to drop the weapon.

"I don't want to hurt yuh, darlin'. Don't fight me and ever thing will be wonderful."

"Let me go! Let me go!"

"You heard the woman, let her go!"

Owen turned his head around to see Thad Larkin and Rebecca standing about five yards away. His sister held something in her arms but he couldn't tell what.

"Go away, both of yuh," Owen circled an arm around Maddie and drew his gun.

"Please, Owen," Rebecca cried. "Don't do this!"

Her brother replied in a loud shout. "I ain't Owen. Git! Yuh don't belong here!"

Larkin spoke in a soft monotone. "OK, Wes. But before we go, there's something we need to leave with you. Something you need."

"I don't need nothin' from you."

Thad studied the situation as best he could. Owen had Maddie in a vise between his right arm and his body. The woman's face was pale with frantic, pleading eyes.

"Maddie is wearing the wooden cross you made, but you don't have the magic box." Thad gently took the box from Rebecca. "I have it right here. What you're doing won't be complete without the box. Let me bring it to you."

A strange, unsettled look of approval appeared in Torveen's eyes. What Larkin had just said made sense to him. "All right, all right, but no tricks. I'll be watchin' yuh."

Larkin walked briskly toward Owen Torveen. As he did he opened the lid of the magic box. "Don't worry, Wes, I'm not trying to fool you."

The sheriff stopped directly in front of Torveen and moved the box to where it was directly under his chin. "See, the box is empty." Larkin moved his hand around inside the box as if to prove the point.

"Maddie, Wes gave you this box as a gift. I think you should get a look too." As he moved the box to Maddie, Larkin turned the lever which flipped the bottom board.

"See there's nothing inside." Thad once again moved his hand inside the box, this time he pulled out the derringer that was fastened to the bottom and fired at Owen.

Owen stumbled backwards, reeling from the force of the bullet. He made a painful cry as he held tightly to his Colt. Thad advanced on him, tossing away the box and the derringer. As Torveen began to point the gun at him, Larkin landed a hard punch on his jaw.

Owen Torveen collapsed to the ground and squirmed in pain. Larkin scooped up Torveen's gun as Rebecca embraced Maddie.

"I need a doctor."

Torveen's words inflamed disgust in Thad Larkin. With all the fine people in the town who needed Fenton Stamford's attention, it seemed wrong for the doctor to have to give time to a murderer who was destined to hang. But Larkin also knew the importance of treating a killer in a just manner.

"Vengeance belongs to the Lord, not me," the sheriff whispered to himself.

Torveen's voice became louder. "Get me a doctor."

"I'll have the ladies get a buckboard for you, Owen. You can't ride in your condition. We should have you into town soon."

A look of intense fanaticism filled Torveen's face. "I'm not Owen, I'm Wes Torveen."

"No, you're not!" Maddie broke away from Rebecca and walked over to where she could look down on the man who had almost killed her.

Desperation now penetrated Torveen's eyes. "Yes I am, Maddie. Remember what I told yuh 'bout a miracle—"

"Shut up!" Maddie's scream sounded harsh and accusing. Torveen shut up.

Maddie turned away from Owen and looked at the man standing beside her. "Reverend Larkin, could you take that phony beard off Owen and wash the ink from his face while Rebecca and I get the buckboard?"

"Ah . . . sure."

"He'll tell people that he's Wes. I don't want anyone to believe him."

Rebecca quietly approached Maddie and placed a hand on her shoulder. "Honey, it's really not that important."

"Yes it is," Maddie's voice was firm. "You see, Wes and I loved each other; for the first time we both felt loved and accepted. For a brief moment we both had a happy future ahead of us."

The woman paused and her next words seemed to come from the deepest part of her soul. "That was the real miracle."

Chapter Twenty-Four

Thad Larkin, Rebecca Torveen, and Fenton Stamford stepped out of the doctor's surgery and into his living room. "Owen will have to stay here for another day or two," Stamford said. "Then we can move him over to the jail."

Rebecca's face was ashen. "I can't believe Owen would do such terrible things. And why would he pretend to be Wes?"

"Like I said earlier, he wasn't pretending," Larkin said.

A stunned curiosity filled Rebecca's eyes. Thad replied to her unasked question. "While I was studying in the East for the ministry, I had several friends who were medical students. They often discussed some famous cases in Europe: cases involving men who became confused about their own identities."

"I read about those cases in medical journals," the doctor responded. "The technical term is 'disassociation.' A person undergoes some terrible event in life. He then begins to cut himself off from his own identity and takes on another identity. These identities can often fight for control of his body."

Rebecca Torveen shivered even though the

room was warm. "You think something like that happened to Owen?"

"Yes," Larkin replied. "Owen always thought of himself as the big brother, the one who had to look out for his two younger siblings."

Rebecca nodded her head. "True enough. I remember hearing father lecture Owen about Wes. If the boys at school picked on Wes, Father expected Owen to join the fight."

"And, from what I hear, Owen did just that." Thad paused for a moment and then continued. "But the lure of being a good friend to the richest boy in the area was too much of a temptation. Owen went along with Josh Franklin's idea of shooting Wes in the leg. That's when the seed was planted."

"I don't quite follow."

"Owen felt a terrible guilt for having set up his brother," Fenton added. "But no one knew about his betrayal except Josh Franklin, who kept quiet. In a way, Owen got away with it, but the guilt inside him grew."

"That guilt was probably spurred by the fact that Owen began to lead a double life," Larkin said. "When the ranch began to lose money, he got involved in a counterfeiting operation with Rob Laverty. He was posing as a legitimate rancher while sinking deeper into criminality."

Everyone went silent for a moment. When Fenton Stamford began to speak, he sounded almost like he was talking to himself. "When Owen had to protect his own interest by joining in the plot to ambush Wes . . . well . . . that pushed him over the edge."

"That's when he became Wes?" Rebecca asked.

"Yes," Larkin said. "His first act as Wes was to kill Stanley Wiggins and Rob Laverty, men who were involved in the ambush. Of course, the real Wes had already killed Ed Horton."

Rebecca inhaled deeply as if recovering from an assault. "But why would Wes, I mean, Owen, shoot at Maddie and me when we were riding with Doctor Stamford to visit Louise Franklin?"

"Self-defense," Larkin quickly replied. "Louise had never seen Maddie before. The one thing they have in common is that Maddie knew Josh when he was a child. Owen was afraid that Louise would talk about that terrible day when he and Josh tried to shoot Wes. In the telling she could have revealed that Owen didn't go for help. So, in this case, Owen posed as Wes while keeping his own identity. It was still important to your older brother that no one would ever know the cruel trick he and Josh had almost pulled on Wes. Owen had to keep Maddie away from Louise."

The young woman pressed her lips together before speaking. "Yes, Louise likes to talk about the past."

"I found that out when I went along with Fenton to visit her. She needed only a little prodding to talk about that day. I'm sure it still eats at her."

"How do the laws . . ." Rebecca's voice began to break and tears began to streak her face. Fenton hastily handed her a handkerchief.

"Thank you." The woman dabbed at her eyes then spoke through a tight throat. "How does the law handle this kind of thing?"

"I can't really answer that," Thad admitted. "But if Owen can be proved insane he will be committed to an institution. He won't hang."

The sheriff immediately regretted his use of the word "hang" but it was too late. "Owen is not going to hang!" Rebecca snapped. "I'll get the best lawyer from the East if I have to!"

The woman pressed her eyes shut, then reopened them. "I'm sorry."

Thad spoke in a quiet voice. "There's nothing to be sorry for and you have every right to get a good lawyer. I only hope that during the trial your brother keeps his identity as Owen."

"That might be very difficult," Fenton Stamford said.

Thad's eyebrows lifted. "Why's that?"

Stamford answered in a quivering voice as if shocked himself by what he was about to say. "That bullet you fired at Owen this morning went directly into his right shoulder and did extensive damage. He'll never be able to use his right arm again."

• • •

Ott Burke sipped the last of his coffee and almost banged the cup on the sheriff's desk. "Lord help the simple folk like me! I was jus' gettin' to like this here job. But if bein' a lawdog means figurin' out people like Owen Torveen, maybe I need to get back to the ranch."

Ott threw up his hands and began to pace about the office. Thad Larkin, who was sitting at the desk, felt a bit guilty about laughing at Burke's frustration. There were better ways to unload the tensions he felt since shooting Owen that morning. He needed to encourage his deputy.

"Ott, you're already proving to be a fine lawman," Larkin said. "And someday, you'll appreciate cases like this which give you a change from drunks and petty crooks."

"Thanks for talkin' me up." The deputy stopped pacing. "You've explained things good, but tell me, how'd you first figure on Owen not bein' what he put on? He sure had the rest of the town fooled."

"Maddie Johnson claimed to have magical powers," Thad answered. "And twice I saw her bring Owen Torveen down by casting one of her spells."

Ott picked up his empty coffee cup and placed it on a small table that stood beside the pot bellied stove. "Yep. Lots of folks saw her knock Owen down at Wes's funeral."

"But she never cast a spell on anyone else except Owen. Since I never believed Maddie was a witch that meant Owen was helping with the deception."

Ott's face beamed with insight. "Owen needed for folks to believe Maddie Johnson was a witch, or, like as not, they'd be wonderin' where all that money she conjured up came from."

"Right!" Larkin exclaimed with approval. "And Maddie knew she had him in a corner."

"Maybe I'll make a good lawdog after all!"

"Right now, you're a lawdog in need of food and rest. Take a few hours off, I'll do the next round alone."

For the next half hour, Larkin tried to busy himself with paperwork. He was happy when Fenton Stamford entered the office.

"Hope I'm not interrupting anything." The doctor spoke in a strong and firm manner but his face reflected fatigue.

Larkin gestured toward the papers on his desk. "I'm too restless for this stuff."

"Rebecca is also pretty restless, but she can't leave her brother yet. She, Brad Myers and Maddie are with Owen. You know, Rebecca and Brad plan to marry soon."

"I didn't know but it doesn't surprise me."

"They plan on Maddie living with them. Rebecca will be deeply involved in running the ranch. They'll need all the help they can get."

"That should work out well."

Fenton Stamford began to fidget with his hands. "We need to talk about some changes right here in town."

"Yes. Let's start looking for a new sheriff. Ott Burke is a terrific deputy but he needs—"

Stamford blurted out, "Let's talk about getting a new pastor for the church and keeping the sheriff we've got."

"What?! We agree—"

"I know what we agreed." Mayor Stamford didn't care to review history. "But this town can't abide another Rob Laverty. Right now, you're calling isn't behind a pulpit, it's behind a badge!"

Mayor Stamford realized his words had slammed Thad Larkin hard. The sheriff's eyes seemed to search the office finding nowhere of comfort to rest.

"I've got to get over to the restaurant to get some food for those fools sitting with Owen." Fenton didn't know why he used the word "fools." He reckoned he was probably thinking more about himself. "Give some thought to what I said. You've got a few days to decide."

After Stamford departed, Larkin shuffled papers for a few more minutes and then gave it up. "Might as well do that round now."

The sheriff started his round by standing on the boardwalk outside of the office and observing the town of Creekside, Arizona. The words Maddie

Johnson had spoken that morning echoed in his mind. *Wes and I loved each other; for the first time we both felt loved and accepted. For a brief moment we both had a happy future ahead of us. That was the real miracle.*

But why did the miracle have to be so fleeting? Thad Larkin had planned on devoting his life to helping people answer questions like that. Now, he wondered if he was up to the job. Maybe the mayor was right. He should stay behind the badge.

Larkin tried to clear his mind. He needed to focus on the work in front of him. Too many fine lawmen had been killed while doing a routine round. He needed to be alert.

Still, troubling thoughts stayed with him as he walked through the dark uncertainty of night.

Louisa May Alcott

Author, Nurse, Suffragette

by Carol Greene

CHILDRENS PRESS ™

CHICAGO

PICTURE ACKNOWLEDGMENTS

Concord Free Public Library—pages 2, 8, 61, 62 (2 photos), 63, 65
Brown Brothers—pages 60, 66
The Bettmann Archive—page 64
Culver Pictures—page 67

Library of Congress Cataloging in Publication Data

Greene, Carol.
  Louisa May Alcott, author, nurse, suffragette.

  Includes index.
  Summary: A biography of the nineteenth-century
American author best known for her autobiographical novel
"Little Women".
  1. Alcott, Louisa May, 1832-1888—Biography—Juvenile
literature. 2. Authors, American—19th century—
Biography—Juvenile literature. [1. Alcott Louisa May,
1832-1888. 2. Authors, American. 3. Nurses.
4. Suffragettes] I. Title.
PS1018.G73   1984   813'.4 [B] [92]   84-5902
ISBN 0-516-03208-9

  2 3 4 5 6 7 8 9 10 R 93 92 91 90 89 88 87 86 85

This book is for my mother, Loretta Greene.

Table of Contents

Chapter 1

WELCOME

Welcome, welcome, little stranger,
Fear no harm, and fear no danger;
We are glad to see you here,
For you sing "Sweet Spring is near."

From TO THE FIRST ROBIN written
by Louisa when she was eight years old

Nothing sang "Sweet Spring is near" when Louisa May Alcott was born. November 29, 1832, was a cold, wintry day in Germantown, Pennsylvania. But baby Louisa was as welcome as that first robin anyway.

Her father, Bronson Alcott, was so excited about her birth that he sloshed a mile down the muddy road to tell his friends, the Haines family. They were so excited that all seven Haines children sloshed back with him to see the new baby.

Then Bronson wrote a letter to Colonel Joseph May, little Louisa's grandfather in Boston:

"Dear Sir,—It is with great pleasure that I announce to you the *birth of a second daughter*. She was born at half-past 12 this morning, on my birthday (33), and is a very fine healthful child, much more so than Anna was at birth,—has a fine foundation for health and energy of character. . . . Abba inclines to call the babe *Louisa May*,—a name to her full of every association connected with amiable benevolence and exalted worth. I hope *its present possessor* may rise to equal attainment, and deserve a place in the estimation of society."

People wrote like that in those days. And Bronson Alcott tended to use even more big words and high ideas than other people did. He was a philosopher with a head full of wonderful visions of how the world could—and should—be.

Bronson, a poor boy, had picked up most of his education on his own as he worked on his father's farm or peddled tin kettles from door to door. Now he was head of his own school in Germantown, a school that his friend Reuben Haines had helped him start. Bronson felt that children should be given a good, sound education, but that lessons should be made interesting, not dull. Mr. Haines, a Quaker, agreed with him, and for a time the school did very well.

Louisa's mother, Abba (short for Abigail) Alcott, was the daughter of an old Boston family, the Mays. She had had a quiet girlhood and then had taught school for a while. Abba met Bronson when he came to visit her brother. They were married in 1830. Louisa's elder sister, Anna, was born in 1831, just three months after the Alcotts came to Germantown.

Bronson's school, Pine Place, was an ideal spot for children. Low hills and clumps of woodland full of birds hugged the square farmhouse with its cedar fence and big garden. The sweet scent of honeysuckle mixed with the sharp tang of pine. Not far away were rivers and streams to walk along and field after field carpeted with wild flowers to pick.

Best of all was the Haines farm, just a bit up the road. Here baby Louisa could toddle under the tall rosebushes and play with the ducks. From the very beginning she was an adventurous little girl who usually wandered farther than she should and had to be bundled back to safety.

Pine Place would have been the perfect place for the Alcott children to grow up. Unfortunately, Reuben Haines had died shortly before Louisa was born, and without his help the school at Pine Place ran into trouble. Some of Bronson's ideas seemed much too strange to his conservative neighbors and, one by one, they took their children out of his school. In March of 1833, Pine Place had to close, and the Alcotts left with sad hearts and happy memories.

For a short time they lived in nearby Philadelphia. But that didn't work out either. So in 1834 the Alcott family boarded a ship for Boston. Shortly after boarding someone noticed that Louisa was missing. Where could she be? Could she have fallen overboard? Everyone began searching for her. They covered the whole ship before they found her—in the engine room—filthy dirty and perfectly happy.

In Boston, Bronson again worked at his dream of running the ideal school. This new one was called the Temple School because it met in the Masonic Temple. Anna was a student there and Abba Alcott helped with the music program. Louisa, however, was allowed to pay only short visits; she had a bad habit of interrupting whatever was going on.

Still, there were plenty of other things to amuse a little girl in busy Boston. Horse-drawn carriages rushed through the streets, bearing beautiful ladies and elegant gentlemen. The town crier strode along, ringing his bell and shouting the latest news. Ragged children chased one another through the alleys, tripping over stray cats as they ran. Louisa loved it all. In fact, one morning at breakfast, she announced to her family, "I love everybody in this whole world."

She found a new group of relatives to love in Boston too. There were her kind Uncle Samuel, her stern Grandfather May, and her pretty Cousin Lizzie. Her mother's family were important people, she learned, especially her mother's great-aunt, Aunt Hancock, who was the widow of John Hancock, the first signer of the Declaration of Independence. Aunt Hancock probably had died before the Alcotts moved to Boston, but Louisa certainly heard plenty of stories about her. The old lady had ruled her family with an iron hand and had done things just as she pleased, including eating her dessert before the rest of her meal because that was the good old-fashioned way.

Louisa also heard the old saying about her mother's family—"The Mays are peppery." She could certainly believe that. Both Louisa and her mother had the fiery May temper.

Two more family members joined the Alcotts during those Boston days. First came baby Elizabeth, born in 1835. Then a little boy was born, but he lived only a short while.

Meanwhile, Louisa kept herself busy and—sometimes—in trouble. She was still quite small when she set out one afternoon to explore Boston all by herself. Of course she got lost, but she didn't cry, not even when it began to get dark. She was a peppery May. So she sat down on a step, put her head on the back of a nice big dog, and fell asleep. The voice of the town crier woke her up.

"Lost," he was shouting, "a little girl, six years old, in a pink frock, white hat, and new green shoes."

"Why, that's me!" Louisa shouted back.

The town crier took her to his home and fed her bread and molasses until her family came for her. That was fun. It wasn't fun, though, the next day to be tied to the arm of a sofa until she had learned her lesson.

But learning her lesson didn't mean that Louisa stayed out of trouble. One day Louisa and her mother went walking on the Common, a big grassy place where Louisa loved to play. Abba Alcott made the mistake of looking away from her daughter for just one instant and—plop!—into the frog pond fell Louisa. Helplessly she struggled, gasping for air, while the grown-ups around her stared in panic. A young black boy didn't panic, though. He jumped right into the pond and rescued the little girl. Then he smiled at her and, before anyone could thank him or even ask his name, he disappeared. Louisa never forgot him.

It must have been about this time—or perhaps even earlier—that she had another experience she never forgot. She was in a kitchen somewhere, the sort of kitchen that had a brick oven with an iron door as part of the fireplace. Suddenly Louisa heard a noise in that oven. She went over and opened the door. Gazing out at her was a face, a terribly thin black face, with fear-haunted eyes. Quickly Louisa slammed shut the door and ran to find her mother.

The man in the oven was a runaway slave, explained Abba Alcott. He had come from a plantation in the South. If the authorities caught him, they'd beat him, put him in chains, and drag him back to his owners. There were many black people like him. People who didn't believe in slavery hid them until they could make their way to freedom and safety in Canada. Louisa must not say a word to anyone about the man she had seen, Abba warned. If she did, not only might he be caught, but the people who had hidden him would be punished too.

Slavery was a burning issue at that time, although it would not erupt into the Civil War until years later. The people of the United States were already divided. To begin with, there were those who owned slaves and those who didn't. Then, even the people who didn't own slaves were split into two groups—those who believed that slavery was all right and those who thought it was dreadfully wrong and should be abolished.

The people who wanted to do away with slavery were known as Abolitionists, and Bronson and Abba Alcott were part of them. So was Bronson's friend, William Lloyd Garrison, who was dragged through the streets by a hysterical mob who wanted to hang him for his beliefs.

Louisa was too young at that time to understand all the details about Abolitionists and slavery. But she understood the most important thing. Slavery was wrong. Black people deserved the same good things that white people had—including freedom and the right to an education.

It was this last belief, firmly held by Bronson too, that ended their stay in Boston for the Alcotts. Bronson was not a man who just talked about his beliefs. He lived them. When Louisa was about seven, Bronson Alcott invited a little black girl to attend the Temple School. The shocked parents of his other students immediately withdrew their children, and the school closed.

Again the family had to move. Bronson had heard about Concord, Massachusetts. A friend, Ralph Waldo Emerson, had told him he would like it there. So the Alcotts packed up and set off for Concord to begin yet another new life.

Chapter 2

THE HAPPIEST DAYS

By the rude bridge that arched the flood,
Their flag to April's breeze unfurled,
Here once the embattled farmers stood
And fired the shot heard round the world.

From CONCORD HYMN
by Ralph Waldo Emerson

Some writers say that they never use people or events from real life in their books. That wasn't true for Louisa May Alcott—at least not all the time. When she wanted to entertain young readers, she often turned to her own life and to events that had happened to her or her relatives or friends.

In *Little Men*, for example, Jo tells the story of a small girl lost in Boston as if it had happened to her. (Many things that happened to Louisa ended up happening to Jo, too.) The house in Concord to which the Alcotts now moved found its way into *Little Women* as Meg's first home.

In real life the house was called the Hosmer Cottage and stood on the edge of town. Louisa and her sisters loved the garden, the fields with a river running through, and the big barn where they could play. It was in that garden that Louisa found the robin to which she wrote her poem. Her mother was so excited about the poem that she told Louisa, "You will grow up a Shakespeare!"

But Louisa did not spend all her time playing and writing poems. Even though she did not go to school much, she had lessons to learn at home from both her father and her mother. Bronson taught his daughters the alphabet by twisting his body into the shapes of the letters, which the girls thought was great fun. Years later, Louisa had Grandpa March use the same method with Demi in *Little Women*.

Louisa worked hard at her lessons—at least most of them—and later wrote:

"I never liked arithmetic nor grammar, and dodged those branches on all occasions; but reading, writing, composition, history, and geography I enjoyed, as well as the stories read to us. . . 'Pilgrim's Progress,' Krummacher's 'Parables,' Miss Edgeworth, and the best of the dear old fairy tales made the reading hour the pleasantest of our day. . . . Walks each morning round the Common while in the city, and long tramps over hill and dale when our home was in the country, were a part of our education, as well as every sort of housework,—for which I have always been very grateful. . . ."

Abba and Bronson Alcott, like other parents of their day, felt it was important for their children to learn lessons about life too. They required that their children study *Pilgrim's Progress* by John Bunyan. *Pilgrim's Progress* tells the story

17

of a man called Christian who struggles through many temptations and hard times until he finally reaches the Celestial City. The teachings in this book became so real to the Alcott girls that they played at being pilgrims themselves, just as the March girls did in *Little Women*.

As they grew older, Louisa and her sisters kept journals, which their parents were free to read at any time. This lack of privacy didn't seem to stop the girls from writing exactly what they felt. In fact, they were pleased when their mother wrote little notes in the journals to help them along.

While they lived in Concord, Abba Alcott wrote to Louisa:

"Dear Daughter,—Your tenth birthday has arrived. May it be a happy one, and on each returning birthday may you feel new strength and resolution to be gentle with sisters, obedient to parents, loving to every one, and happy in yourself.

"I give you the pencil-case I promised, for I have observed that you are fond of writing, and wish to encourage the habit.

"Go on trying, dear, and each day it will be easier to be and do good. You must help yourself, for the cause of your little troubles is in yourself; and patience and courage only will make you what mother prays to see you,—her good and happy girl."

It is remarkable that Abba Alcott could spend as much time as she did teaching her children what she thought they needed to know to be "good and happy" people. Her own life certainly wasn't easy at this time. The family was very poor. Making ends meet, plus housework, cooking, sewing, and caring for her family, kept Abba busy every minute of the day. To top things off, a new baby was born to the Alcotts in Concord, another little girl, called May.

Bronson tried to support his growing family by raising food in the garden, working on his neighbors' farms, and chopping wood for a dollar a day. But making money was definitely not one of his talents.

Abba had no stove, so she cooked the family's meals at the fireplace. Often the only foods they had were fruits, vegetables, boiled rice, and graham meal. Even so, for a while they ate just two meals a day, taking the third to a family even poorer than they. Abba insisted on just two things—enough milk to keep her children healthy and enough wood to keep them warm in winter. Even those things were hard for impractical Bronson to manage sometimes.

One snowy evening the woodshed was almost bare and Abba was worried sick. Then, like a miracle, a neighbor sent a load of wood. Abba sighed with relief. But her relief didn't last long. Soon Bronson came tromping into the house, announcing that he had given the wood to a poor family with a sick baby.

What about his own family? His own baby? Oh, he wasn't worried. They'd be all right. Abba must have been ready to scream. Just then there was a knock at the door. Another neighbor had decided to sent them a load of wood too. "I told you that we would not suffer," Bronson informed Abba.

Her parents' generosity to less fortunate people must have made a powerful impression on Louisa. It was about this time that she was invited to visit some older relatives in Providence. While she was there, she met some neighborhood children who told her they didn't get much to eat at home.

At once Louisa raided her hostess's pantry and loaded the children up with all the food they could carry. When her relatives found out, Louisa received a stern lecture and was sent to the attic. There she sat, trying to figure out what she had done wrong. Finally a young man in the family came up, explained things as best he could, and wiped away her stormy tears.

Both Louisa and Anna understood about poverty. They realized that finances were troubled in their home, but they didn't worry too much about such things then. There were many things to do that didn't cost money. Later Louisa wrote, "Those Concord days were the happiest of my life. . . ."

Sometimes the girls had strawberry parties among the trees. Sometimes they made up plays and acted them out in the old barn. Sometimes they played with neighbor children, including the little Emersons. Most glorious of all, as far as Louisa was concerned, were the times she spent running free through the woods and fields.

"I always thought I must have been a deer or a horse in some former state," she wrote, "because it was such a joy to run. No boy could be my friend till I had beaten him in a race, and no girl if she refused to climb trees, leap fences, and be a tomboy.

"My wise mother, anxious to give me a strong body to support a lively brain, turned me loose in the country and let me run wild, learning of Nature what no books can teach. . . .

"I remember running over the hills just at dawn one summer morning, and pausing to rest in the silent woods, saw, through an arch of trees, the sun rise over river, hill, and wide green meadows as I never saw it before.

"Something born of the lovely hour, a happy mood, and the unfolding aspirations of a child's soul seemed to bring me very near to God; and in the hush of that morning I always felt that I 'got religion,' as the phrase goes. A new and vital sense of His presence, tender and sustaining as a father's arms, came to me then, never to change through forty years. . . ."

In the spring of 1842, Bronson received an invitation to visit some people in England. They shared his ideas about education and wanted to honor him. He couldn't afford to go, but his friend, Ralph Waldo Emerson, found the money for him. Emerson possibly thought Bronson needed the trip to cheer him up after the sad times with his own schools.

So Bronson set off and, according to his letters, had a

marvelous time. Meanwhile, Abba struggled to keep her family going at home. Most likely she borrowed money from relatives to do it. Once again, Bronson was lost in his world of ideas and had completely forgotten practical problems.

Bronson returned to Concord in late summer. With him he brought three men, a boy, and an idea. The men and the boy were to stay with the Alcotts through the winter. The idea was to change their lives yet again.

Chapter 3

THE KINGDOM OF LOVE

Here is the land,
Shaggy with wood,
With its old valley,
Mound and flood.
But the heritors?—
Fled like the flood's foam.
The lawyer, and the laws,
And the kingdom,
Clean swept herefrom.

From HAMATREYA
by Ralph Waldo Emerson

Bronson's idea was based on a philosophy called transcendentalism. He believed that people could live together in love and peace if they would just work at it and let their spirits rule them instead of being ruled by the selfish desires of their bodies. A number of other people, both in England and in the United States, shared that idea. Ralph Waldo Emerson was one of them. He explained transcendentalism in a little book called *Nature*.

Once again Bronson wasn't happy just thinking or writing

about an idea. He wanted to live it. The Alcotts and their English guests would find some land, he explained. As soon as spring came, they would all move there and live together in a perfect little world. They would show love to everyone and everything. Of course they would be vegetarians.

Abba Alcott must have spent some worried hours wondering how all this would work out. Yet it *was* a magnificent plan, and Bronson was so happy and excited about it. So she said nothing and, when a farm was found near Harvard, Massachusetts, Abba rolled up her sleeves and prepared to move again.

They called the farm Fruitlands because of the apple trees already growing there, and the ones they meant to plant. Although Mr. Emerson didn't move in with them, he did help with finances and watched the experiment with great interest. "The sun and the evening sky do not look calmer than Alcott and his family at Fruitlands," he wrote in his journal on July 8, 1843. "Young men and young maidens, old men and women, should visit them and be inspired." Then he added a practical note: "They look well in July; we will see them in December."

Things were still going well in September, at least as far as Louisa was concerned. In her journal she poured out her moods and the events of the day.

"September 1st.—I rose at five and had my bath. I love cold water! Then we had our singing-lesson with Mr. Lane

24

[one of the Englishmen, who taught the children]. After breakfast I washed dishes, and ran on the hill till nine, and had some thoughts,—it was so beautiful up there. Did my lessons,—wrote and spelt and did sums; and Mr. Lane read a story, 'The Judicious Father'. . . .

"We had bread and fruit for dinner. I read and walked and played till supper-time. We sung in the evening. As I went to bed the moon came up very brightly and looked at me. I felt sad because I have been cross today, and did not mind Mother. I cried, and then I felt better. . . ."

Louisa and her sisters had to sleep in the attic because the rest of the small red house was crammed with transcendentalists. The ceiling was so low that the girls must have bumped their heads more than once. But they didn't seem to mind. Besides, according to Louisa, the rain "made a pretty noise on the roof."

Even though they were too young to understand all the talk, the little girls apparently caught some of the grownups' excitement about the "grand work" at Fruitlands, as Mr. Lane called it. And the philosophers did try to teach them a few things. "Father asked us what was God's noblest work," wrote Louisa. "Anna said *men*, but I said babies. Men are often bad; babies never are."

Once Mr. Lane asked the children to write down the virtues they wanted more of. "Patience, obedience, industry, love, generosity, respect, silence, perseverance, self-denial," wrote Louisa. He then asked which vices they wanted fewer of; her reply was, "Idleness, impatience, selfishness, wilfulness, impudence, activity, vanity, pride, love of cats."

Perhaps the part of transcendentalism that Louisa understood best was its respect for nature. She loved cats and all other animals, as well as trees, flowers, water, and the wind rushing over them all. But just to see and feel these things were not enough for her. Like any budding writer, she had to put them into words.

"I made a verse about sunset," she wrote in her journal.

"Softly doth the sun descend
To his couch behind the hill,
Then, oh, then, I love to sit
On mossy banks beside the rill.

"Anna thought it was very fine," she continued, "but I didn't like it very well." Even budding writers must learn to criticize their own work.

Sometimes the girls played at being fairies in the woods, complete with homemade gowns and paper wings. On Elizabeth's eighth birthday, they hung presents from a tree and had a parade to the tree, singing to the music of Mr. Lane's violin.

Of course there was plenty of work to be done too, and the children had their share of tasks. Louisa ironed, cleaned, husked corn, and helped take care of little May. Sometimes she and Anna prepared a whole meal by themselves.

No matter how much the girls did, their mother still looked tired. None of the men seemed to realize that Abba was the only grown woman around to do all the jobs that were considered "women's work" in those days. Not that she complained very often. She loved her husband dearly and was willing to make tremendous sacrifices for his happiness. Once or twice, however, even her patience gave out.

Occasionally visitors came to Fruitlands to see how Bronson's experiment was working. One of these visitors innocently asked if there were any beasts of burden on the place. Abba looked him right in the eye. "Only one woman," she said.

Once the men even left her with their work to do too. They had sown and tended their crops carefully and everything had grown well. Just when it was time to harvest the barley, the men were invited to a conference where they were to explain transcendentalism. The philosophers simply couldn't pass up an opportunity like that. The barley would wait for a few days, they thought, and off they went.

The barley might have waited, but the weather didn't. A day or so after the men left, a storm blew up. Quickly Abba marshaled her army of children. They needed that crop, she explained, to make it through the winter. Rain would ruin it. She would spread her good linen sheets on the ground. The children were to harvest the crop into bags, baskets, or whatever they could find and then dump it onto the sheets, which could be dragged into the barn.

Frantically they worked as lightning split the sky and thunder rumbled. Back and forth they ran with the sheaves until their legs trembled with weariness and their arms ached. It was an impossible task for one woman and a few children. Still, by the time the first drops fell, most of the barley was in the barn.

So much work and love and sacrifice should have made the great experiment work. But what should happen isn't always what does. By her birthday in November that year, Louisa knew that something was wrong—dreadfully wrong. It wasn't just her mother's exhausted, frightened face that told her. The men were acting strangely too.

Some left Fruitlands because the work was too hard and the weather too cold. Others began talking more and more about crops and money. Mr. Lane had gone to visit the Shaker village across the river and kept mentioning how much better their idea worked. The Shakers also believed in a simple, peaceful life. In their community men lived in one dormitory and women in another. The Shakers didn't think men and women should marry and have families. Many of the children in the village were orphans whom the government had given the Shakers to care for. Even these children stayed in separate dormitories.

Maybe the Shakers had the right idea, mused Mr. Lane. Maybe Mr. Lane had a right to be concerned. He had spent much of his own money on Fruitlands—far more than anyone else—and it was beginning to look as if his investment was a failure. He was also worried about his son William. The boy had been ill with a fever for a long time.

Unfortunately, Charles Lane chose the wrong person to blame for his troubles—Abba. "Her pride is not yet eradicated," he wrote to a friend in England, "and her peculiar maternal love blinds her to all else." Peculiar Abba—to care more about her children than about an idea!

At last the truth came out. Mr. Lane wanted Bronson to send Abba and the girls away. He wanted Fruitlands to be run as the Shaker village was, with no husbands, wives, or families. And Bronson did not know what to do.

At least Bronson Alcott was fair enough to ask his family how they felt about all this. Even after they told him, he still could not decide. On December 10, Louisa wrote in her journal:

"I did my lessons and walked in the afternoon. Father read to us in dear Pilgrim's Progress. Mr. L. was in Boston and we were glad. In the eve father and mother and Anna and I had a long talk. I was very unhappy and we all cried. Anna and I cried in bed, and I prayed God to keep us all together."

Then, suddenly, the decision was made. Mr. Lane and his son left Fruitlands and the Alcotts remained—alone and poor, but still together—in the red farmhouse. What a relief the girls must have felt! But their troubles weren't over yet.

Bronson felt that his idea—his magnificent plan for a kingdom of love—had died. With it, a part of him died too. He became very ill and for days lay in his bed, unable to eat or even to speak. The girls must have wondered whether they were going to lose him after all.

Once again, Abba showed her great strength. Patiently she nursed her husband and cared for her children as the winter winds and snow howled outside the drafty old house. Stubbornly she kept working at her own little kingdom of love. And, slowly, Bronson began to recover.

As soon as Bronson was well enough to travel, Abba's brother, kind Uncle Samuel, stepped in and found a house that the Alcotts could rent in nearby Still River. They would be warmer there and not so far from help.

Not much is known about that short stay in Still River, except that the children seemed happy enough. After a while, Bronson began to work again, chopping wood and doing chores for neighbors. The family was still desperately poor, but Louisa and her sisters were used to poverty. At least they still were a family. That was enough for them.

Chapter 4

A PLAN FOR LIFE

I hope that soon, dear mother,
You and I may be
In the quiet room my fancy
Has so often made for thee. . .

From TO MOTHER written by
Louisa when she was ten years old

In November of 1844, the Alcotts moved again. (They moved twenty-nine times during the first twenty-eight years of Louisa's life.) Abba Alcott had inherited some money from her father, to which the generous Mr. Emerson added five hundred dollars. At last the Alcotts were able to buy a home of their own in Concord.

Their new home was a small house on the Lexington road in the southeast part of town. Bronson called it Hillside. He built a terrace on the hill in back of the house. The terrace turned out to be the perfect spot for the children to play their favorite game, Pilgrim's Progress.

It was Abba, however, who came up with the improvement that meant the most to Louisa. For quite a while now, the girl had been longing for a room of her own.

"Dearest Mother,—" she wrote in a note in her journal. "I have tried to be more contented, and I think I have been more so. I have been thinking about my little room, which I suppose I shall never have. I should want to be there all the time, and I should go there and sing and think."

Later her mother responded: "Patience, dear, will give us content, if nothing else. Be assured the little room you long for will come, if it is necessary to your peace and well-being. Till then try to be happy with the good things you have. . . ."

Even while she was preaching patience, Abba's busy mind was spinning plans. The property at Hillside included several outbuildings—sheds, a barn, and a wheelwright's shop. Clever Abba had that shop cut in two and the parts attached to the ends of the house.

Thanks to her mother's creativeness, several months after she was thirteen Louisa could write: "I have at last got the little room I have wanted so long, and am very happy about it. It does me good to be alone, and Mother has made it very pretty and neat for me. My work-basket and desk are by the window. . . . The door that opens into the garden will be very pretty in summer, and I can run off to the woods when I like."

Running in the woods was still important to Louisa. She had grown into a tall, slender girl with dark brown hair and lively gray eyes. Those long legs needed all the exercise they could get and sometimes led their owner into mischief that shocked and embarrassed quiet Anna.

During part of this period in Concord, Louisa and Anna went to a real school. On the way one day, they and their friend Clara Gowing saw a horse and sleigh in front of a neighbor's house. Just like that, Louisa leaped into the driver's seat. Clara scrambled after her and the two girls drove around as fast as they could, while Anna stared in dismay. Then Louisa returned the sleigh and they all went on to school.

In spite of the outbursts of mischief, Louisa was growing more serious too. At thirteen she was old enough to hate the poverty that weighed on her family and to think a bit about the future.

"I have made a plan for my life," her journal shows, "as I am in my teens, and no more a child. I am old for my age, and don't care much for girl's things. People think I'm wild and queer, but Mother understands and helps me. I have not told any one about my plan; but I'm going to *be* good. I've made so many resolutions, and written sad notes, and cried over my sins, and it doesn't seem to do any good! Now I'm going to *work really*, for I feel a true desire to improve, and be a help and comfort, not a care and sorrow, to my dear mother."

By "help and comfort" Louisa meant improving the family's financial situation too. She wanted her mother to have that quiet room she had written about in her poem. She wanted Bronson to be free of the debts that swarmed around him like bees. She wanted Anna and May to have a chance someday to get ahead in the world. And she wanted Elizabeth, who was not a strong child, to have all the physical care she might need.

When she was only twelve, Louisa had put out a sign announcing that she was a dolls' dressmaker. She actually did earn some money this way. Her hats for dolls "were the rage at one time," she wrote later, "to the great dismay of the neighbors' hens, who were hotly hunted down, that I might tweak out their downiest feathers to adorn the dolls' headgear." Of course such a young girl couldn't make much money. Even so, the resolution that Louisa made took root deep in her heart and stayed with her the rest of her life.

Meanwhile, she and her sisters managed to have a great deal of fun without spending any money at all. Both Anna and Louisa loved drama with a passion, and Anna actually was a good actress. Louisa was the playwright. It was from her pen that the plays began to pour.

Louisa dreamed up dashing heroes—such as Duke Roderigo—beautiful heroines, and languishing princesses. When the plays were finished, Louisa ransacked the ragbag and whipped together splendid costumes. Of course all the sisters had to take part in the performances, which were held in the barn, and all the friends had to be invited. It was an inexpensive way to entertain, and all who attended declared that they had had a good time.

Not only did imagination often take the place of money for the Alcott girls, it sometimes led them into hilarious situations. One day Emerson brought a famous transcendentalist, Margaret Fuller, to visit Abba and Bronson. Miss Fuller admired Bronson's theories of education and was eager to meet his own "model children."

A moment later the girls appeared, screeching around the corner of the house. May, dressed as a queen, rode in a wheelbarrow, pulled by the horse, Louisa, and driven by Anna. Gentle Elizabeth, as the dog, was barking as loud as she could. All at once they saw the guests. There was a sudden silence. Then Louisa tripped, pulling her sisters down on top of her in a shrieking, laughing heap.

"Here," said Abba dramatically, "are the model children, Miss Fuller." (That event, slightly changed, showed up years later in *An Old-Fashioned Girl*.)

The wonderful old barn was also headquarters for the Pickwick Club, made up entirely of Alcott girls. The most important project of these Pickwickians was a newspaper, for which Anna wrote sentimental little stories and Louisa penned poems dripping with emotion. The girls also created a post office on the hill and used it to exchange flowers, letters, and books.

The plays, the Pickwick Club, and the post office all eventually found their way into *Little Women*, as did many other adventures from this time in Louisa's life. She didn't set her story at Hillside; instead she used Orchard House, where the family lived later. But when she needed characters and events with which to entertain children, she turned to the people and happenings of one of the happiest periods of her own life.

Meanwhile, Bronson was still not doing much to earn a living for his family. Even so, he was happy in Concord too. Many other people there shared his belief in transcendentalism, including Emerson, who now lived just a little way up the road.

Another young transcendentalist named Henry David Thoreau had built a cabin by Walden Pond on Emerson's property. Thoreau was busy writing a book about his thoughts and experiences. That book, *Walden*, became a classic of American literature. One summer, when he needed to earn a little cash, Thoreau tutored the Alcott girls.

Bronson, however, rarely did anything so practical. He simply never accepted the fact that he and money lived in the same world.

"Mr. Alcott," Abba once wrote in her journal, "cannot bring himself to work for gain; but we have not yet learned to live without money or means."

Once someone gave Bronson ten dollars to buy Abba a warm shawl, which she badly needed. He walked all the way to Boston to get it. Once in the city, he passed a bookshop, where he saw several books he wanted. Bronson didn't make a decision to buy the books instead of the shawl. He simply forgot that such things as shawls existed. When he got home, loaded down with books, his daughters reminded him. Then he was so sorry for what he had done that they couldn't help but forgive him.

Mr. Emerson continued to do all he could to help the Alcotts along. He gave Abba the best advice he could dredge up on how to manage with little or no money. And he let Louisa use his library to her heart's content. Sometimes he suggested that she read a particular book or two. At the same time, she was always free to choose any others she wanted as well.

One day, when she was fifteen, Louisa picked up a volume by the German writer Goethe. The book, *Goethe's Correspondence with a Child*, contained letters written to the poet when he was almost sixty by a young girl, Bettina von Arnim, who thought she was in love with him.

At once Louisa's lively imagination went to work. She wanted to be a Bettina too—and what better Goethe could she find in the neighborhood than dear Mr. Emerson? "So I wrote letters to him," she explained years later, "but never sent them; sat in a tall cherry-tree at midnight, singing to the moon till the owls scared me to bed; left wild flowers on the doorstep to my 'Master,' and sung Mignon's song under his window in very bad German."

Fortunately, Mr. Emerson had no idea that any of this was

going on. When Louisa told him, long after she had grown up, they both enjoyed a good laugh.

It may be that Mr. Emerson was one of the few people who knew of Louisa's secret dream to help her family financially. When she was sixteen, he suggested that she start her own school in the barn. He would send his children to it, and he was sure other neighbors would too.

Louisa turned out to be a good teacher and— like all good teachers—learned a lot from her students too. She never really liked teaching though. It forced her to sit still too long. Still, money was money, and goodness knows the Alcotts needed all they could get. So Louisa ignored her restless legs and taught.

Her favorite pupil was Emerson's little daughter Ellen. It was for Ellen that Louisa wrote her first children's stories, short tales about nature that she later called "flower fables." She would scribble them down, read them to Ellen, and then toss them on the stack of manuscripts, along with her stories and plays about noble heroes and captive maidens.

It may seem strange that Louisa never became angry with her father or criticized him for not doing more for his family. She didn't. She accepted him just as he was and loved him with all her heart. Love isn't always blind, though. Many years later, someone asked Louisa what her definition of a philosopher was. She didn't even have to think. "My definition is of a man in a balloon, with his family and friends holding the ropes which confine him to earth and trying to haul him down." She loved her father. But she understood him too.

So did Abba Alcott. But Abba also felt responsible for the whole family, as well as for the debts that were piling up. One day a friend from Boston stopped by to see her and found Abba with tears on her face. "Abby Alcott, what does this mean?" demanded the friend.

Then it all poured out like a flood—the worry, the pain, and the fear. The friend went back to Boston determined to help however she could. Before long a letter came to Abba from a group of women called the South End Friendly Society. They wanted her to come to work for them. She would visit poor people and decide who should get help—and how much—from different charities.

Abba had a long talk with her family. Then she wrote her letter of acceptance. It almost broke her heart to have to take money for the sort of work she loved to do as a volunteer. Yet she couldn't afford the luxury of saying no. Besides, the women's idea was a new one and a good one. It would do a great deal to help poor people.

So the Alcotts got ready to leave Concord and move to Boston. For Louisa this meant leaving behind the woods and fields and some of the people she loved. It also meant leaving behind her childhood.

Chapter 5

WORKING HANDS

I am glad a task to me is given
To labor at day by day;
For it brings me health, and strength, and hope,
And I cheerfully learn to say,—
"Head, you may think; heart, you may feel;
But hand, you shall work alway!"

From A SONG FROM THE SUDS
by Louisa May Alcott

Louisa did not write in her journal for quite a while after the family moved to Boston. When she did begin again in the spring, she was seventeen, and she tells why:

"Boston, May, 1850.—So long a time has passed since I kept a journal that I hardly know how to begin. Since coming to the city I don't seem to have thought much, for the bustle and dirt and change send all lovely images and restful feelings away. Among my hills and woods I had fine free times alone, and though my thoughts were silly, I daresay, they helped to keep me happy and good. . . .

"This summer, like the last, we shall spend in a large house (Uncle May's, Atkinson Street), with many comforts about us which we shall enjoy, and in the autumn I hope I shall have something to show that the time has not been wasted. Seventeen years have I lived, and yet so little do I know. And so much remains to be done before I begin to be what I desire,—a truly good and useful woman.

"In looking over our journals, Father says, 'Anna's is about other people, Louisa's about herself.' That is true, for I don't *talk* about myself; yet must always think of the wilful, moody girl I try to manage, and in my journal I write of her to see how she gets on. . . . My quick tongue is always getting me into trouble, and my moodiness makes it hard to be cheerful when I think how poor we are, how much worry it is to live, and how many things I long to do I never can.

"So every day is a battle, and I'm so tired I don't want to live; only it's cowardly to die till you have done something.

"I can't talk to any one but Mother about my troubles, and she has so many now to bear I try not to add any more. I know God is always ready to hear, but heaven's so far away in the city, and I so heavy I can't fly up to find Him."

Poor Louisa! Most young girls go through such periods of depression and write or think such thoughts. In Louisa's case, it seems as though she really did have good reasons to feel sad and "heavy." Abba's job did not pay well and required dreadfully hard work. Bronson was holding "conversations" for which people paid a small admission fee to hear him talk about his ideas. He loved this work and

41

apparently did help a lot of young people with what he said. Unhappily, his income was too small to do much for the young people in his own family.

(Once a friend of the family, Ednah Cheney, heard him insist at one of these "conversations" that a diet of vegetables "would produce unruffled sweetness of temper and disposition." Suddenly a voice behind her said, very quietly, "I don't know about that. I've never eaten any meat, and I'm awful cross and irritable very often." It was Louisa.)

Louisa and Anna did all they could to earn money. Sometimes they taught small children and sometimes just looked after them. They did sewing for other people and helped with the chores at home. May went to school and Elizabeth was in charge of housekeeping. Louisa once called her "our angel in a cellar kitchen."

It must have been very difficult for Louisa to see girls her own age dressed up in their finery, riding in carriages or sauntering from shop to shop in search of some new trinket. Worst of all must have been the thought that even the future didn't look any brighter for her or her family. Louisa still burned with her dream of lifting them all to a better life, a dream that seemed no closer to coming true.

In July of 1850 she wrote about her mother: "I often think what a hard life she has had since she married,—so full of wandering and all sorts of worry! . . . I think she is a very brave, good woman; and my dream is to have a lovely, quiet home for her, with no debts or troubles to burden her. But I'm afraid she will be in heaven before I can do it."

That summer on Atkinson Street brought a fresh load of trouble to the Alcotts. Kind Abba invited some poor immigrants into the garden one day and fed them. The immigrants turned out to have smallpox, and all the Alcotts caught it. None of the girls was very sick, but Bronson and Abba were. In those days people were terrified of smallpox— with good reason—and no one would come near the family, not even a doctor. So Louisa and Anna nursed their parents themselves. Eventually, Abba and Bronson recovered.

For a while it seemed to Louisa that she might be able to help her family by writing plays and acting in them. "Anna wants to be an actress, and so do I," she wrote in August of 1850. "We could make plenty of money perhaps, and it is a very gay life. Mother says we are too young, and must wait. A. acts often splendidly. I like tragic plays, and shall be a Siddons if I can. [Sarah Siddons was a famous actress.] We get up fine ones, and make harps, castles, armor, dresses, water-falls, and thunder, and have great fun."

Once again Louisa's imagination rescued her from her doldrums. As she taught her small pupils or bent over her sewing, she let her mind spin away at plots. Then, in her spare moments, she wrote down her plays. They were not great drama, but they certainly bristled with adventure, excitement, and every romantic notion Louisa had ever read about. *Bandit's Bride, The Captive of Castile or The Moorish Maiden's Vow*, and *The Rival Prima Donnas* all flowed from her pen. For a while it even seemed as if *The Rival Prima Donnas* would be put on in a real theater. Much to Louisa's disappointment, that project fell through.

Very well, she thought, if she couldn't be a famous dramatist, she would find some other way to earn more money.

As part of her work with the South End Friendly Society, Abba Alcott had begun an employment agency to help poor women find jobs. One day a clergyman came to the house, looking for someone to be a companion for his invalid sister. All this companion would have to do, he said, was read aloud to Miss Eliza and do a few light household tasks. It sounded like the perfect job, and Louisa talked her mother into letting her take it.

Off she marched one wintry day, ready to begin her month's trial period. It didn't take her long to find out that the clergyman had lied. She was never once asked to read aloud. Instead her duties included carrying coal from the shed and water from the well, splitting kindling, sifting ashes, shoveling paths in the snow, cleaning, and scrubbing. Louisa was furious. But she had agreed to a month, so she gritted her teeth and dug in.

Then one evening the clergyman began to scold her for not doing enough. In addition to everything else, he expected her to black his boots! Louisa said no. The clergyman fussed and fumed. She still said no. Much later that night she glanced out into the hall and saw him doing the job himself. That was the best moment of the month for her.

Finally the month was up and she announced that she was leaving. Miss Eliza cried and begged so hard that Louisa agreed to stay on until they hired someone else. For three weeks longer she toiled. Two applicants came, took one look, called Louisa a fool, and left again. When the third one appeared, Louisa lost no time. She was leaving, she said. Period. At the last moment, Miss Eliza pressed a little purse into her hand and Louisa fled.

"So I left the house," she wrote later, "bearing in my pocket what I hoped was, if not liberal, at least an honest return for seven weeks of the hardest work I ever did. Unable to resist the idea to see what my earnings were, I opened the purse—and beheld four dollars! I have had many bitter moments in my life, but one of the bitterest was then, when I stood on the road that cold windy day, with my little pocketbook open, and looked from my chapped, grimy, chilblain hands to the paltry sum that had been considered enough to pay for the labor they had done."

When her family found out what had happened, they were horrified. Peace-loving Bronson swore that if ever he saw that clergyman again, he'd shake him till his teeth rattled. Poor as they were, the Alcotts refused to accept the insult of that four dollars. Louisa sent it back.

45

During that same period, though, Louisa had a happy surprise. Her father found one of the "flower fables" she had written for Ellen Emerson in Concord and gave it to a friend in publishing. The friend read it, liked it, printed it, and paid Louisa five dollars. Secretly she must have been very proud, although she treated it as a joke.

"My first story was printed, and $5 paid for it," she wrote. "It was written in Concord when I was sixteen. Great rubbish! Read it aloud to sisters, and when they praised it, not knowing the author, I proudly announced her name."

Louisa summed up 1853 in one short journal entry: "In January I started a little school. . . about a dozen in our parlor. In May, when my school closed, I went to L. as second girl. I needed the change, could do the wash, and was glad to earn $2 a week. Home in October with $34 for my wages. After two days' rest, began school again with ten children. Anna went to Syracuse to teach; Father to the West to try his luck,—so poor, so hopeful, so serene. God be with him! Mother had several boarders, and May got on well at school. Betty [Elizabeth] was still the home bird, and had a little romance with C. . . ."

Bronson returned from his lecture tour to the West in February of 1854. He arrived late one night, and Abba and the girls flew downstairs in their white nightgowns to greet him. After everyone had fed and fussed over the weary traveler, young May asked, "Well, did people pay you?"

Bronson smiled sadly, opened his pocketbook, and showed them one dollar bill. "Only that!" he said. "My overcoat was stolen, and I had to buy a shawl. Many promises were not kept, and traveling is costly; but I have opened the way, and another year shall do better."

"I shall never forget how beautifully Mother answered him," Louisa wrote later, "though the dear, hopeful soul had built much on his success; but with a beaming face she kissed him, saying, 'I call that doing *very well*. Since you are safely home, dear, we don't ask anything more.'

"Anna and I choked down our tears, and took a little lesson in real love which we never forgot, nor the look that the tired man and the tender woman gave one another. It was half tragic and half comic, for Father was very dirty and sleepy, and Mother in a big nightcap and funny old jacket."

That same year, when Louisa was twenty-two, a publisher brought out in book form all the little stories she had written for Ellen. The book was called *Flower Fables* and earned Louisa thirty-two dollars. She slipped a copy into her mother's Christmas stocking with this note: "Dear Mother,—Into your Christmas stocking I have put my 'first-born,' knowing that you will accept it with all its faults (for grandmothers are always kind), and look upon it merely as an earnest of what I may yet do; for, with so much to cheer me on, I hope to pass in time from fairies and fables to men and realities."

Meanwhile, she stuck with the "fairies and fables" and

sold a number of stories to various newspapers. "I want more fives," she'd told Anna earlier, "and mean to have them too."

In June of 1855, Cousin Lizzie Wells decided it was high time Louisa had a vacation and invited her to spend the summer in Walpole, New Hampshire. Louisa must have felt like a bird let out of a cage.

"So glad to run and skip in the woods and up the splendid ravine," she wrote.

"Helped cousin L. in her garden; and the smell of the fresh earth and the touch of the green leaves did me good.

"Up at five, and had a lovely run in the ravine, seeing the woods wake. Planned a little tale which ought to be fresh and true, as it came at that hour and place. . . ."

In July the rest of the Alcotts came to Walpole too. They had been invited to live—rent-free—in a friend's house, and it seemed just too good an opportunity to pass up. "Plays, picnics, pleasant people, and good neighbors," wrote Louisa.

By September both she and Anna realized that it was up to them to earn more money if the family were to make it through the winter in Walpole. Anna received an offer to teach at an asylum in Syracuse and took it. For a while Louisa waited to see if anything like that would turn up for her. It didn't, and so she was forced to make one of the hardest decisions she had yet made.

Louisa knew that she couldn't earn enough money by her

writing alone, and there were no other jobs to be had in Walpole. So, even though her family was the most important thing in the world to her, for their sakes she packed her little trunk, took twenty dollars she had earned and some stories she had written, and set off for Boston, all alone, to make whatever fortune she could.

Chapter 6

PARTINGS

Sitting patient in the shadow
Till the blessed light shall come,
A serene and saintly presence
Sanctifies our troubled home.
Earthly joys and hopes and sorrows
Break like ripples on the strand
Of the deep and solemn river,
Where her willing feet now stand.

From OUR ANGEL IN THE HOUSE
by Louisa May Alcott

That first winter alone in Boston is pretty well summed up in Louisa's journal entry for December of 1855: "H. and L. W. very kind, and my dear cousins the Sewalls take me in. I sew for Mollie and others, and write stories. C. gave me books to notice [review]. Heard Thackeray [author of *Vanity Fair*]. Anxious times; Anna very home-sick. Walpole very cold and dull now the summer butterflies have gone. Got $5 for a tale and $12 for sewing; sent home a Christmas-box to cheer the dear souls in the snow-banks."

All winter she wrote, taught, and sewed. "Sewing won't

make my fortune," she told her journal, "but I can plan my stories while I work, and then scribble 'em down on Sundays."

Bronson took one of those stories to a friend of his who was editor of a famous magazine. "Tell Louisa to stick to her teaching," advised this man. "She is never going to be a writer."

"I will *not* stick to my teaching," replied Louisa when she heard what he had said. "I *will* be a writer. And I will write for his magazine too." (Some years later she did just that.)

Lectures and visits with friends and relatives brightened some of those gray winter days. But no matter how busy she was, Louisa could never entirely forget her worry for her family back "in the snow-banks" of Walpole.

In June she went home to them "to find dear Betty very ill with scarlet-fever caught from some poor children Mother nursed. . . ." Those children had been living over a cellar where pigs had been kept. Their landlord, a deacon in his church, repeatedly refused to clean the place until Abba Alcott threatened to sue him. "Too late to save two of the poor babies," wrote Louisa, "or Lizzie and May from the fever. An anxious time. I nursed, did house-work, and wrote a story a month through the summer."

May recovered completely, but when fall came, Elizabeth was still very weak. Although Louisa must have wanted desperately to stay and go on nursing her, she realized that she could do more for her family in Boston. So in October she wrote: "Made plans to go to Boston for the winter, as there is nothing to do here, and there I can support myself and help the family. C. offers 10 dollars a month, and perhaps more. L. W., M. S., and others, have plenty of sewing; the play *may* come out, and Mrs. R. will give me a sky-parlor for $3 a week, with fire and board. I sew for her also.

"If I can get A. L. to governess I shall be all right.

"I was born with a boy's spirit under my bib and tucker. I *can't wait* when I *can work*; so I took my little talent in my hand and forced the world again, braver than before and wiser for my failures."

Years later Louisa wrote alongside this journal entry "Jo in N.Y." Anyone who has laughed and cried with Jo March over her adventures in her attic room—her "sky-parlor"—can imagine Louisa's life at that time.

In spite of her "boy's spirit" and bravery, it cost Louisa something to leave home that autumn. "I don't often pray in words," she wrote, "but when I set out that day with all my worldly goods in the little old trunk, my own earnings ($25) in my pocket, and much hope and resolution in my soul, my heart was very full, and I said to the Lord, 'Help us all, and keep us for one another,' as I never said it before, while I looked back at the dear faces watching me, so full of love and hope and faith."

Once again Louisa began writing, sewing, and—eventually—teaching. Her pupil was a little invalid girl, Alice L., who could not go to regular school. Even though Louisa still did not much like teaching, she enjoyed the hours she spent with Alice in a big fine room. Her own "sky-parlor" was a bit bare after all.

Other people helped make the long winter bearable. Kind Cousin Lizzie Wells gave her tickets for a series of lectures on Italian literature, plus a cloak to wear to them. Another cousin gave her a pass to the theater. Best of all—the thing that seemed to do Louisa the most good that winter—was her friendship with Mr. Parker.

Theodore Parker was a Unitarian minister—and a transcendentalist. He hated "war, slavery, drunkenness, and the subjugation of women" and was known as "the most crowd-drawing preacher in Boston."

Like Bronson Alcott, Mr. Parker lived out his beliefs, as well as preached them. Once he hid a runaway slave woman in his house and sat writing his sermon with a pistol beside him in case the authorities tried to take her back. Another time he married two runaway slaves who were about to be smuggled to England by the Abolitionists. Armed men guarded the door while he performed the ceremony. When it was over, he gave the fugitives two wedding gifts—a Bible "for the defense of your soul" and a Bowie knife "for the defense of your body."

Louisa admired Mr. Parker tremendously for his actions and beliefs. She was also grateful to him for his kindness to her personally. Each Sunday evening the Parkers held a reception at their house. Some of the great people of the time attended these gatherings, and Louisa was told to come whenever she liked.

She never said much at these entertainments. It was enough to sit in a corner and listen and stare. But more than once these outings—and the warmth of Mr. Parker himself— were enough to get her through a difficult week. "He is like a great fire," she wrote, "where all can come and be warmed and comforted. Bless him!"

In November May came to Boston too. She was to stay with an aunt and study drawing, music, and French. Louisa was delighted to see her and put aside whatever pennies she could to buy pretty things for her. It never seemed to bother Louisa that May had a much easier life than she herself did. May loved beauty and had artistic talent. To Louisa it was only right that she be given all the help she needed to get ahead.

Louisa's twenty-fourth birthday was a homesick time for her, even though friends gave her a little party. Then when she got home to her room that evening, she found a pin and a letter from her father and letters from her mother and Elizabeth. That was what she had needed, and she went to bed happy.

January brought a momentous event. Louisa received her first new silk dress, a gift from generous Cousin Lizzie

Wells. It wasn't a small gift either. Women's fashions in those days required yards and yards of fabric. "I felt as if all the Hancocks and Quincys [her ancestors] beheld me as I went to two parties in it on New Year's eve," wrote Louisa.

In the spring Louisa went back to Walpole, pleased at having done all she had wanted to—"supported myself, written eight stories, taught four months, earned a hundred dollars, and sent money home."

In June she wrote: "All happy together. My dear Nan [Anna] was with me, and we had good times. Betty was feeble, but seemed to cheer up for a time. The long, cold, lonely winter has been too hard for the frail creature, and we are all anxious about her. I fear she may slip away; for she never seemed to care much for this world beyond home."

In July Bronson's mother came for a visit. Louisa was pleased to get to know the "sweet old lady" who, at eighty-four, was still "very smart, industrious, and wise." That visit gave Louisa an idea for a story about her father's life. "The trials and triumphs of the Pathetic Family would make a capital book," she wrote. She even had her title, *The Cost of an Idea*. Somehow that particular book never got written.

By August Elizabeth was worse, and Abba Alcott took her to the seashore for a month. It was clear to everyone that Elizabeth would not survive another fierce New Hampshire winter. Therefore plans were made to move back to Concord where the sick girl would be closer to medical care. Besides, the whole family would feel better being near Mr. Emerson again.

Hillside was no longer available. Living in it were the already famous author Nathaniel Hawthorne and his family. From somewhere (Mr. Emerson?) Abba found enough money to buy a ramshackle old house farther up the same road. Its official name was Orchard House, but Louisa preferred to call it Apple Slump.

A great deal of work had to be done before the family could move in. For the time being, they rented part of another house, fixed up a room there as comfortably as they could for Elizabeth, and trekked out each day to Apple Slump to clean and polish, paint and paper, prune and plant.

In November Elizabeth seemed a little better again. At least she enjoyed watching her sisters get ready for the plays they put on at a nearby boys' school, which belonged to a friend of theirs. "I lead two lives," Louisa wrote. "One seems gay with plays, etc., the other very sad,—in Betty's room; for though she wishes us to act. . . the shadow is there, and Mother and I see it. Betty loves to have me with her; and I am with her at night, for Mother needs rest. Betty says she feels 'strong' when I am near."

In January of 1858, she continued: "Lizzie much worse; Dr. C. says there is no hope. A hard thing to bear; but if she is only to suffer, I pray she may go soon. She was glad to know she was to 'get well,' as she called it, and we tried to bear it bravely for her sake. We gave up plays; Father came home; and Anna took the housekeeping, so that Mother and I could devote ourselves to her. Sad, quiet days in her room, and strange nights keeping up the fire and watching the dear little shadow try to wile away the long sleepless hours without troubling me. She sews, reads, sings softly, and lies looking at the fire,—so sweet and patient and so worn, my heart is broken to see the change. I wrote some lines one night on 'Our Angel in the House.' "

In February Elizabeth rallied again and the Alcotts allowed themselves to feel a flicker of hope. Then, on March 14, Louisa wrote: "My dear Beth died at three this morning, after two years of patient pain. Last week she put her work away, saying the needle was 'too heavy,' and having given us her few possessions, made ready for the parting in her own simple, quiet way. For two days she suffered much, begging for ether, though its effect was gone. Tuesday she lay in Father's arms, and called us round her, smiling contentedly as she said, 'All here!' I think she bid us good-by then, as she held our hands and kissed us tenderly. Saturday she slept, and at midnight became unconscious, quietly breathing her life away till three; then, with one last look of the beautiful eyes, she was gone."

The funeral service was held on Monday. Her family and friends sang Elizabeth's favorite hymn, "Come, Ye Disconsolate." Years later Louisa quoted the last line of that hymn in *Little Women*: "Earth hath no sorrow that Heaven cannot heal." To hear it summed up the comfort she clung to, that God had set her sister free and "Beth was well at last."

In April Anna announced to her family that she was engaged to handsome, quiet John Pratt. "So another sister is gone," wrote Louisa. It was hard for her not to be bitter at this new turn of events. Of course she loved Anna and wanted her to be happy. If John Pratt was the one to give her that happiness—well, all right. Still her family was all she had, and it hurt her terribly to see it breaking up. Later, though, she was able to write, ". . . we gained a son and brother, and Anna the best husband ever known."

In June repairs were finally finished, and the Alcotts moved into Orchard House. With them, however, they brought a new mountain of debts, including Elizabeth's medical bills.

"We won't move again for twenty years if I can help it," wrote Louisa in August. "The old people need an abiding place; and now that death and love have taken two of us away, I can, I hope, soon manage to care for the remaining four."

All summer she had been scribbling away at her stories and "simmering" novels as she did the housework. By October, though, she had become completely discouraged. Heavy thoughts weighed her down as she walked one day over the milldam and looked at the water below. Beth was gone and Anna was leaving. No matter how hard she worked, she couldn't earn enough. For just a moment she was once again so tired that she didn't want to live.

Then Louisa's usual courage flamed to life again. "There is work for me, and I'll have it!" she thought. Home she went to pack her little trunk and set off once more for Boston.

A few years after her twentieth birthday, Louisa's first book, *Flower Fables*, was published.

Louisa, in 1879, was the first woman to register as a voter in Concord, Massachusetts. This is how Concord looked in about 1865.

Two men Louisa May Alcott greatly respected were Henry David Thoreau (left) and Ralph Waldo Emerson (below).

After Louisa's sister May died, her daughter Lulu Nieriker came to live with Louisa.

Abba Alcott in Orchard House

Left: Bronson Alcott on the steps
of the chapel that served as lecture
room for his school at Orchard House

Orchard House in Concord, Massachusetts

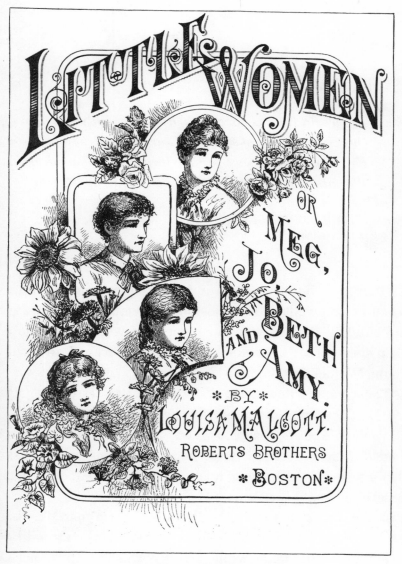

An 1880 edition of *Little Women*

Chapter 7

BETTER TIMES

The world lies fair about us, and a friendly sky above;
Our lives are full of sunshine, our homes are full of love;
Few cares or sorrows sadden the beauty of our day;
We gather simple pleasures like daisies by the way.

From THE CHILDREN'S SONG
by Louisa May Alcott

At first it didn't seem as if better times were coming. When Louisa went back to Boston, her heart still felt heavy and she had no idea whether or not she would find a job. Then she heard Mr. Parker preach a sermon on "Laborious Young Women."

"Trust your fellow-beings," he said, "and let them help you. Don't be too proud to ask, and accept the humblest work till you can find the task you want." It was just what Louisa needed to hear. Her spirits perked up, and she went to ask Mrs. Parker if she knew of a job. Mrs. Parker felt sure that something would turn up.

On her way home from the Parkers, Louisa met Mrs. L., mother of her former pupil, Alice. Alice had been attending a regular school for a while, but she wasn't happy there.

Maybe—just maybe—the family would hire Louisa to teach her again.

The next day a friend of the Parkers offered her a job. Would she like to work at the Girls' Reform School in Lancaster? She would be sewing and mending ten hours a day. Poor Louisa! Of course she wouldn't like it. It would be like going to prison herself. But she didn't feel she could say no. So she said all right—unless Mrs. L. wanted her.

Evening came and Louisa packed her bag, ready to set out for Lancaster. Then there was a knock at the door. It was a messenger with a note from Mrs. L. She wanted Louisa back—and at the same salary as before.

"So away to my little girl with a bright heart!" wrote Louisa. "For with tales, and sewing for Mary, which pays my board, there I am fixed for the winter and my cares over."

Now that life had taken an upward swing, Louisa could look back on the troubles of the past with a clearer mind. "Now that Mother is too tired to be wearied with my moods, I have to manage them alone," she wrote, "and am learning that work of head and hand is my salvation when disappointment or weariness burden and darken my soul.

"In my sorrow I think I instinctively came nearer to God, and found comfort in the knowledge that he was to help when nothing else could. . . .

"I feel as if I could write better now,—more truly of things I have felt and therefore *know*. I hope I shall yet do my great book, for that seems to be my work, and I am growing up to it."

The stories Louisa was writing now were tales of adventure, full of passion, romance, and strange happenings. She knew they weren't very good and even called them "trash and rubbish." But publishers wanted them and were willing to pay for them, so she scribbled on. Still, deep in her heart, she yearned to write something of which she could be proud.

"Some day I'll do my best," she told her journal, "and get paid for it."

In January Abba became ill, and Louisa went home for a week to nurse her. Once again she found out what a good nurse she was. "Wonder if I ought not to be a nurse?" she thought to herself. Then she hurried back to Boston.

In April, her work with Alice finished, Louisa returned to Concord. May was home again too, after studying art at the School of Design and doing very well. "No doubt now what she is to be, if we can only keep her along," wrote Louisa.

During the month of May, she nursed Cousin Lizzie Wells and in June took in two children to board and teach. Meanwhile, people began to talk of war. Even peaceful folk such as Henry Ward Beecher and Ralph Waldo Emerson thought it must come if slavery were to be abolished. Louisa felt excited about living at a time when such things were happening. She had never forgotten the boy who had pulled her out of the frog pond or the runaway slave hidden in an oven.

"Glad I have lived to see the Anti-slavery movement," she wrote. "Wish I could do my part in it."

For the rest of the year she wrote away, finally having a story accepted by the *Atlantic Monthly*, an important magazine that paid her fifty dollars. In February of 1860, a publisher refused one of her stories "because it is anti-slavery." Louisa must have felt both proud and disappointed at that.

About this time, Bronson got a job as superintendent of schools in Concord. He loved the work, the children loved him, and he even earned a small salary. No wonder Louisa called 1860 "A Year of Good Luck."

In March Mr. Emerson asked her to write a song for the Concord schoolchildren, which she did gladly. Four hundred little students sang "The Children's Song" at their school festival, and later seventy of them paraded over to the Alcott home to serenade Bronson and Louisa.

On May 23, 1860, Anna and John Pratt were married at Orchard House. Abba's brother, Uncle Samuel, performed the ceremony and afterwards everyone danced on the lawn. "I mourn the loss of my Nan, and am not comforted," said Louisa. She must not have meant that too seriously, though, because she also wrote: "Then, with tears and kisses, our dear girl, in her little white bonnet, went happily away with her good John; and we ended our first wedding. Mr. Emerson kissed her; and I thought that honor would make even matrimony endurable. . . ."

Louisa's attitude toward marriage has puzzled many people. Did she really think it as unpleasant as she sometimes said? She had once received a proposal of marriage from a man with quite a bit of money. But, she told her mother, she didn't love him. Then she must not marry him, advised Abba.

Just a month before Anna's wedding, Louisa wrote in her journal about another experience: "Had a funny lover who met me in the cars, and said he lost his heart at once. Handsome man of forty. A Southerner, and very demonstrative and gushing, called and wished to pay his addresses; and being told I didn't wish to see him, retired, to write letters and haunt the road with his hat off. . . . He went at last, and peace reigned. My adorers are all queer."

Another time, after visiting Anna and John in their new home, she wrote : "Very sweet and pretty, but I'd rather be a free spinster and paddle my own canoe."

Louisa believed in love. Her stories are filled with all kinds of love—between parents and children, brothers and sisters, friends, cousins, and husbands and wives. Louisa herself loved her own family dearly—and felt responsible for them. Perhaps that is why she never married. Perhaps she never found anyone with whom she felt she could share that love and responsibility. No one really knows.

That same spring Theodore Parker died, and in June Louisa went to Boston for his memorial service. "I was very glad to have known so good a man, and been called 'friend' by him," she wrote.

Meanwhile, she was hard at work on a novel, called *Moods*. "Genius burned so fiercely," she wrote in August, "that for four weeks I wrote all day and planned nearly all night, being quite possessed by my work. I was perfectly happy, and seemed to have no wants. . . . Daresay nothing will ever come of it; but it *had* to be done, and I'm the richer for a new experience."

After those four weeks, she put *Moods* away to "settle" for a while and went back to her stories. The *Atlantic* bought still more of them and she was able to get a few more necessities for her family. Times must still have been hard, because in December she wrote: "A quiet Christmas; no presents but apples and flowers. No merry-making for Nan and May were gone, and Betty under the snow. But we are used to hard times, and, as Mother says, 'while there is a famine in Kansas we mustn't ask for sugar-plums.'

"All the philosophy in our house is not in the study; a good deal is in the kitchen, where a fine old lady thinks high thoughts and does kind deeds while she cooks and scrubs."

In February of 1861, Louisa attacked *Moods* again and worked in a frenzy for about three weeks. She couldn't eat, didn't sleep much, and left her desk only once a day to go for a run. Her worried mother brought her cups of tea and her proud father brought her apples and cider. Louisa barely noticed them as she sat there, wearing the old red and green wrap she called her "glory cloak."

Then her body quite firmly said, "Stop!" Her head felt dizzy and her legs shaky. She couldn't sleep even when she wanted to. So Louisa stopped. She read her family what she had written. Her mother said it was wonderful. Anna, who was visiting, said she was proud of her. Bronson said, "Emerson must see this."

Another month passed. When April came, something happened that drove even her beloved *Moods* out of Louisa's mind for a while. Fort Sumter was fired upon and the Civil War began. Concord was one of the first towns to send its sons off to Washington. Louisa said, "At the station the scene was very dramatic, as the brave boys went away perhaps never to come back again."

Secretly she was fuming that she wasn't one of those brave boys. All that women could do at that point in the war was to sew for the soldiers, and that didn't seem enough to her. But she sighed, picked up her needle, and did the best she could.

In May Anna found out that Louisa, who had spent long hours sewing for her sisters too, was wearing their old cast-offs. Anna got together with May and the two of them sent Louisa a new wardrobe. That sort of thing didn't happen to her very often, and she called it "a beautiful surprise." More happy moments came in July, when she spent a month in the White Mountains with Cousin Lizzie.

In January of 1862, an old friend of her father's, Elizabeth Peabody, suggested that Louisa open a kindergarten in Boston. Miss Peabody was very interested in the whole idea of kindergartens, which had begun in Germany. Louisa was beginning to feel restless anyway, so once again she swallowed her dislike of teaching and agreed.

Soon she was set up in the Warren Street Chapel with a room and twelve little pupils. Unfortunately, the job didn't pay enough for her to rent a room, not even a "sky-parlor." Instead, she had to "board around," staying with one family after another. That must have been terribly hard for a sensitive person like Louisa.

"Hate to visit people who only ask me to help amuse others," she wrote, "and often longed for a crust in a garret with freedom and pen. I never knew before what insolent things a hostess can do, nor what false positions poverty can push one into."

By April Louisa had decided to commute between Concord and Boston every day. "Forty miles a day is dull work; but I have my dear people at night, and am not a beggar."

In spite of her teaching and the forty miles a day, Louisa managed to write another story, for which she was paid thirty dollars. That seemed to settle the matter for her. Now she could earn more by her writing than by her teaching. So why teach? May agreed to finish up the last month of her sister's contract, and Louisa went home.

At home she sewed for the soldiers and for the baby that Anna and John were expecting and wrote to her heart's content. "L. . . . [one of her publishers] wants more than I can send him," she wrote. "So . . . I reel off my 'thrilling tales.' . ."

News from the war was bad at this time, and Louisa never quite managed to accept the needle as her only weapon. "I . . . long for battle like a war horse when he smells powder," she wrote. "The blood of the Mays is up!"

Her journal entry for November of 1862 begins with two simple statements: "Thirty years old. Decided to go to Washington as a nurse if I could find a place." A nurse. She had always thought she would be a good one. Why not try now—and do her part for the anti-slavery movement at the same time?

"I want new experiences," she wrote, "and am sure to get 'em if I go." She certainly would—and those experiences would change her life in more ways than one.

Chapter 8

DUTY'S CHILD

When I remember with what buoyant heart,
Midst war's alarms and woes of civil strife,
In youthful eagerness thou didst depart,
At peril of thy safety, peace, and life,
To nurse the wounded soldier, swathe the dead . . .
I press thee to my heart as Duty's faithful child.

From TO LOUISA MAY ALCOTT
by Bronson Alcott

On December 11, 1862, Louisa received a note from a Miss H. M. Stevenson. It told her to start for Georgetown, just outside Washington, D.C., the next day. There she would serve as nurse at the Union Hotel Hospital. A Mrs. Ropes, of Boston, was matron of the hospital. It was a "hard place," where help was badly needed.

"I was ready," Louisa wrote in her journal, "and when my commander said 'March!' I marched. Packed my trunk, and reported in B[oston] that same evening."

At the last moment of farewell, the whole Alcott family broke down in tears. "I realized that I had taken my life in my hand, and might never see them all again," wrote Louisa.

She spent the next day running all over Boston. There was a railway pass to be obtained, parcels to pick up, a veil to buy, and a tooth to have filled. Someone gave her some old clothes, and her relatives, the Sewalls, gave her money for herself and the "boys." Then, at 5 P.M., Louisa climbed on a train and began her long journey.

Later she wrote: "I said my prayers as I went rushing through the country white with tents, all alive with patriotism, and already red with blood.

"A solemn time, but I'm glad to live in it; and am sure it will do me good whether I come out alive or dead."

Louisa arrived in Georgetown late one evening. The hospital had once been a hotel—and not an especially good or clean one. Now it was crammed with cots and mattresses and all the paraphernalia of an emergency medical center.

In those days, hospitals and hospital care left a great deal to be desired, and military hospitals were sometimes the worst of all. It was not an easy life that Louisa faced. But she was as qualified as anyone else for the job. Most hospitals were staffed by untrained nurses. In England, Florence Nightingale was just beginning to graduate young women from that unheard-of thing—a school for nurses. Louisa's fellow staff members gave her a warm welcome when she appeared that December night.

She was shown to her room, a bare chamber that she would share with two other nurses. A narrow fireplace supplied the only warmth, and many of the windowpanes were broken and let in the wintry air. As she lay in bed, Louisa could hear the scuttling of cockroaches and the scratching of rats in the closet. But none of that mattered. She was there to do a job, and she couldn't wait to begin.

"On the morrow began my new life by seeing a poor man die at dawn," she wrote, "and sitting all day between a boy with pneumonia and a man shot through the lungs. A strange day, but I did my best; and when I put mother's little black shawl round the boy while he sat up panting for breath, he smiled and said, 'You are real motherly, ma'am.' I felt as if I was getting on."

She spent her first two days in that twenty-bed ward, where most of the patients suffered from typhoid, pneumonia, or measles. On the third day, forty ambulances pulled up at the hospital, filled with soldiers who had been wounded at the Battle of Fredericksburg. It was then that Louisa met the full horror of war.

She was assigned to the former hotel's ballroom, which was now a ward for the most seriously wounded. These men had fought for days in rain and mud, only to face a bloody defeat because of a mistake on some official's part.

"The first thing I met was a regiment of the vilest odors that ever assailed the human nose," wrote Louisa later. "There they were! our 'brave boys' as the papers justly call them, for cowards could hardly have been so riddled with shot and shell, so torn and shattered, nor have borne suffering for which we have no name, with an uncomplaining fortitude, which made one glad to cherish each as a brother.

"In they came, some on stretchers, some in men's arms, some feebly staggering along propped on rude crutches, and one lay stark and still with a covered face, as a comrade gave his name to be recorded before they carried him away to the dead-house. . . ."

Louisa stood and stared. She longed to help, but had no idea where to begin. Then the nurse in charge thrust a basin, towels, sponge, and cake of brown floor-scrubbing soap in her arms. "Come, my dear, begin to wash as fast as you can," she said. "Tell them to take off socks, coats, and shirts, and scrub them well, put on clean shirts, and the attendants will finish them off and lay them in bed."

Louisa fought down her nervousness and turned to the nearest patient, an Irishman covered with dirt. At first she dabbed at him as gently as she could, terrified that she would hurt him. With a twinkle in his eye, the man said, "May your bed above be aisy, darlin', for the day's work you are doin'." Louisa burst out laughing, and the Irishman joined in. From then on, though always gentle, she "scrubbed away like any tidy parent on a Saturday night."

After this positive beginning, Louisa settled into a routine. "Up at six, dress by gaslight, run through my ward and throw up the windows, though the men grumble and shiver;

but the air is bad enough to breed a pestilence; and as no notice is taken of our frequent appeals for better ventilation, I must do what I can."

Next she went to breakfast "with what appetite I may." Louisa felt sure that the food must be left over from the Revolutionary War—"pork just in from the street; army bread composed of sawdust and saleratus [baking soda]; butter, salty as if churned by Lot's wife; stewed blackberries that looked like preserved cockroaches; tea—three dried huckleberry leaves to a quart of water, flavored with lime." Obviously her sense of humor had not deserted her.

"Till noon I trot, trot, giving out rations, cutting up food for helpless 'boys,' washing faces, teaching my attendants how beds are made or floors are swept, dressing wounds, taking Dr. F. P.'s orders (privately wishing all the time that he would be more gentle with my big babies), dusting tables, sewing bandages, keeping my tray tidy, rushing up and down after pillows, bed-linen, sponges, books, and directions, till it seems as if I would joyfully pay down all I possess for fifteen minutes' rest."

At noon the soldiers received their dinners. Then some slept, some read, and some wanted Louisa to write letters for them. She enjoyed doing this, but, she said, "The answering of letters from friends after some one had died is the saddest and hardest duty a nurse has to do."

Supper arrived at five. After eating, the patients settled

down to read newspapers, gossip, and wait for the doctors' last rounds of the day. Evening doses of medication were handed out. Then ". . . at nine the bell rings, gas is turned down, and day nurses go to bed. Night nurses go on duty, and sleep and death have the house to themselves."

It sounds like an exhausting, heartbreaking sort of life. But Louisa did not regret coming. In January of 1863 she wrote in her journal: "I never began the year in a stranger place than this: five hundred miles from home, among strangers, doing painful duties all day long, and leading a life of constant excitement in this great house, surrounded by three or four hundred men in all stages of suffering, disease, and death. Though often homesick, heartsick, and worn out, I like it, find real pleasure in comforting, tending, and cheering these poor souls who seem to love, to feel my sympathy though unspoken, and acknowledge my hearty good-will, in spite of the ignorance, awkwardness, and bashfulness which I cannot help showing in so new and trying a situation. The men are docile, respectful, and affectionate, with but a few exceptions; truly loveable and manly many of them."

Some, of course, touched her heart more deeply than others. Very early in her stay, she offered to feed a man who had eaten none of his meal. "Thank you, ma'am," he said, but shook his head. "I don't think I'll ever eat again, for I'm shot in the stomach. But I'd like a drink of water if you ain't busy."

Louisa hurried off to get him one. But by the time she returned, the man had died. "It seemed a poor requital," she wrote, "for all he had sacrificed and suffered . . . for there was no familiar face for him to look his last upon; no friendly voice to say Good-bye, no hand to lead him gently down into the Valley of the Shadow. . . ."

Then there was Billy, the twelve-year-old drummer boy. Louisa found him shaking with chills and crying in the night. "I dreamed that Kit was here," he sobbed, "and when I waked up he wasn't."

Louisa soothed him and then sat down to listen to his story. He had marched with the men in General Burnside's army and done his duty bravely, small as he was. Sure, it was hard, but he had his friend Kit, the soldier who looked after him, teased him, and gave him good advice.

Billy had already caught a fever when the Battle of Fredericksburg began. He was much too sick to play his drum. All he could do was lie in his tent, burning with fever and worrying about Kit who was somewhere in the thick of the fighting.

Suddenly he heard the sound of men running. It was a retreat—they had lost the battle! Terrified, the little boy lay in his tent until a pair of strong arms scooped him up and he heard Kit's voice in his ear.

For miles the two traveled on together, at first on foot, then in an ambulance. During some of this time Billy slept, exhausted by his fever. Now and then he heard some other soldier offer to take him from Kit's arms. But Kit would not let him go.

At last Billy woke up at the hospital door. Strange arms reached out for him now and in panic he asked for Kit. Kit was gone, gently explained another soldier. He had been wounded himself all the while he had carried Billy. Finally—well, he just couldn't go on any longer.

Billy took the news of his friend's death as bravely as any grown-up soldier. He hadn't even cried—not until the dream came and he had had to face the loss of Kit all over again.

Billy eventually got well and was sent home, leaving behind his story of a friendship that only death could end. Louisa heard many such stories in her wards and came to know many brave men. Most dear to her was John Sulie, a blacksmith from Virginia. John was so big that he had to have a special bed. His body had once been strong and powerful. Now, shot in the lung and in the back, he could not lie down without dreadful agony.

Louisa wrote that John was "the prince of patients; and though what we call a common man in education and condition, to me is all I could expect or ask from the first gentleman in the land. Under his plain speech and unpolished manner I seem to see a noble character, a heart as warm and tender as a woman's, a nature fresh and frank as any child's. He is about thirty, I think, tall and handsome, mortally wounded, and dying royally without reproach, repining, or remorse."

It was Louisa who had to tell John that he was dying. He bore this news as bravely as he bore his wounds. At night Louisa sat beside him whenever her duties permitted. John Sulie died holding her hand.

Louisa wrote to her family about him—and about Billy and Kit and the others. She had no time to polish those letters, only to sketch in words, as quickly as she could, the stories of tremendous courage and love that she found in the midst of war's pain and squalor. They were true pictures, written from the heart. Perhaps it eased her heart, too, to write them.

A month of "bad air, food, and water, work and watching" had begun to take its toll on her, but she fought to keep her health as long as she could. Whenever possible, she chose night duty over the day shift so that she could go for a morning run. Unfortunately, it was a battle she could not win. A "sharp pain in the side, cough, fever, and dizziness" caused the doctors to order her to her room for rest and treatment. Mrs. Ropes, the matron, had the same symptoms—those of typhoid pneumonia—and was already close to death.

Louisa stayed in her room and sewed for the "boys," read, wrote letters, and slept. The sleep didn't seem to do her much good, though, because it brought such awful dreams. Three doctors faithfully climbed the stairs each day to care for her, but nothing they did seemed to help. "They want me to go home," wrote Louisa, "but I *won't* yet."

At last someone told the dying matron what was going on. She issued orders to send for Bronson at once. Louisa awoke from a feverish dream to find her father entering her room. Still she wouldn't go home. If she could just rest a while longer, she insisted, she was certain she would be well enough to go back to work.

Then, on January 21, she felt "very strangely" and agreed to go home. Friends and former patients came to see her off, including Miss Dorothea Dix, who brought her a basket filled with wine, tea, and medicine, plus a blanket, a pillow, a fan, and a New Testament with her own initials inside.

Dorothea Dix was superintendent of nurses for the Union Army, a valiant fighter for improved care of the wounded. She had also done much to improve civilian hospitals, as well as conditions in prisons, and was responsible for the establishment of state hospitals for the mentally ill. Louisa said later that the "D. D." in the New Testament meant more to her than if it had stood for Doctor of Divinity.

It took a day and a night to get Louisa as far as Boston. She said she felt "half asleep, half wandering, just conscious that I was going home." She was too sick to travel on to Concord that night, so they stayed at the Sewalls' where she "had a sort of fit; they sent for Dr. H., and I had a dreadful time of it."

By the next afternoon, however, she was able to go on. "Just remember seeing May's face at the depot," she wrote, "Mother's bewildered one at home, and getting to bed in the firm belief that the house was roofless, and no one wanted to see me."

Louisa was delirious for three weeks. She would never forget some of the "strange fancies" that haunted her during this time. Perhaps the worst was being sure that she had married a Spanish man of whom she was desperately frightened. She finally decided to talk to the pope about him. Later her family told her that she really did get up and make a speech in something that sounded like Latin.

Even after the delirium had passed, Louisa was sick for a long time. Her parents stayed with her night and day, the doctor visited daily, and May read or sang to her to pass away the hours.

It wasn't until April that she began to feel like herself again. She was still thin, all her beautiful hair had been cropped off, and—although she didn't realize it then—her health had been permanently damaged. In financial terms, she had earned just ten dollars for her work as a nurse. But in other ways, she had gained a great deal. And she knew it.

"Had some pleasant walks and drives, and felt as if born again, everything seemed so beautiful and new," Louisa wrote one April day. "I hope I was, and that the Washington experience may do me lasting good. To go very near to death teaches one to value life, and this winter will always be a very memorable one to me."

Chapter 9

LITTLE WOMEN

Four little chests all in a row,
  Dim with dust and worn by time:
Four women, taught by weal and woe
  To love and labor in their prime;
Four sisters parted for an hour,—
  None lost, one only gone before,
Made by love's immortal power
  Nearest and dearest evermore.

From LITTLE WOMEN
by Louisa May Alcott

Several pleasant things happened in 1863 while Louisa was getting well. On March 28 Anna gave birth to a baby boy. According to Louisa, the whole family screamed for about two minutes when Bronson came in with the news. May and Louisa at once came up with a name guaranteed to satisfy all the relatives: Amos Minot Bridge Bronson May Sewall Alcott Pratt. Fortunately for the baby, Anna and John settled for Frederic Alcott Pratt.

It took Louisa a while to start writing after her illness. She felt as if she had to learn how all over again. One thing she did work on was a poem she had begun one night as she watched by John Sulie's cot. Called "Thoreau's Flute," it was written to honor her old friend and teacher who had died the previous spring.

When she finished the poem, Louisa showed it to her family and friends. Mrs. Hawthorne took it to the editor of the *Atlantic* who immediately wanted to publish it. Louisa was delighted. Not only did she get paid (ten dollars), but many people praised the poem.

Perhaps one of the highest compliments came when Bronson was visiting the poet Henry Wadsworth Longfellow. At that time, poems were printed in the *Atlantic* without the names of their authors. Longfellow picked up his copy and told Bronson he wanted him to read a poem about Thoreau that Emerson had written. Imagine Bronson's pride as he said, "Louisa wrote that."

In April a Mr. Sanborn asked Louisa to arrange for publication in the *Commonwealth* some of the letters she had written while nursing. Louisa came up with three "Hospital Sketches." To her great surprise, people loved them. "Witty and pathetic," they said and bought up copies of the paper as fast as they could. "More!" they demanded. So Louisa gave them more.

Two different publishers—Redpath and Roberts Brothers—asked if they might bring out the sketches in book form. Louisa chose Redpath, little dreaming that one day in the future it was Roberts Brothers that would help make her fortune.

On July 25, "my first morning-glory bloomed in my room,—a hopeful blue,—and at night up came my book in its new dress." The first edition sold well and earned Louisa forty dollars. Furthermore, both publishers and the public began to sit up and take notice of Louisa May Alcott.

"If there was ever an astonished young woman, it is myself," she wrote in October, "for things have gone so swimmingly of late I don't know who I am. A year ago I had no publisher, and went begging with my wares; now *three* have asked me for something, several papers are ready to print my contributions, and F. B. S. says 'any publisher this side of Baltimore would be glad to get a book.' There is a sudden hoist for a meek and lowly scribbler, who was told to 'stick to her teaching.' ..."

Such moments are good for a writer's soul. But, as usual, Louisa was thinking very little of herself. "I may yet 'pay all the debts, fix the house, send May to Italy, and keep the old folks cosey,' ..." she continued. By January of 1864 she could see that 1863 had been a big year for her. She had earned almost six hundred dollars by her writing. (All she spent on herself was less than a hundred for some badly needed bed-room furniture.)

Now Louisa was eager to get on with the writing. From her pen flowed fairy tales and sketches, not to mention the "thrillers" that still paid well. But her heart was back with her novel, *Moods*. She loved this story of a spoiled rich girl and sent it to publisher after publisher. "It's too long," they all said. "Can't you make it shorter?"

Finally Louisa figured out a way to do as they asked and spent another of those feverish periods rewriting the book. "We'll take it," said a publisher and Louisa promptly forgot "weariness, toothache, and blue devils."

The blue devils returned, though, when the publisher sent her the proofs for *Moods*. Now the chapters seemed "small, stupid, and no more my own." The original version was better—as she had thought all along. "What is true for your own private heart is true for others," Emerson told her, which comforted her a little. So she went back to her stories and to another book, which she later called *Work*.

Moods came out on Christmas Eve of 1864 and sold well at first. Even the reviews were good, although papers in England complained that they didn't understand "transcendental literature." "My next book shall have no *ideas* in it," Louisa wrote in her journal, "only facts, and the people shall be as ordinary as possible; then critics will say it's all right."

In April of 1865, she went to Boston to help celebrate the end of the Civil War. The "grand jollification" was cut short, though. "On the 15th in the midst of the rejoicing came the sad news of the President's [Abraham Lincoln's] assassination, and the city went into mourning. . . . Saw the great procession, and though few colored men were in it, one was walking arm in arm with a white gentleman, and I exulted thereat."

By June Louisa was back at her "rubbishy tales" and having her first taste of a new problem. "Strangers begin to come," she wrote, "demanding to see the authoress, who does not like it, and is porcupiny."

On June 24 (Elizabeth's birthday), Anna had another boy, John Pratt, Jr. "A fine, stout, little lad," Louisa called him, "who took to life kindly, and seemed to find the world all right."

Sometimes it was hard for Louisa herself to "find the world all right." Along with her writing, she still did huge amounts of housework because, as she wrote to Anna, "May gets exhausted with work, though she walks six miles without a murmur." It was not like Louisa to complain, especially about her beloved May. But her health was still not all it should be and the family debts continued to hang over her, no matter how much she wrote.

"It is dreadfully dull, and I work so that I may not 'brood,'" she continued in the same letter to Anna. "Nothing stirring but the wind; nothing to see but dust; no one comes but rose-bugs; so I grub and scold at the 'A.' [*Atlantic*] because it takes a poor fellow's tales and keeps 'em years without paying for 'em. If I think of my woes I fall into a vortex of debts, dishpans, and despondency awful to see. So I say, 'every path has its puddle,' and try to play gayly with the tadpoles in *my* puddle, while I wait for the Lord to give me a lift, or some gallant Raleigh to spread his velvet cloak and fetch me over dry shod."

In July something happened to give her that lift. She was invited to go to Europe as traveling companion to a young invalid, Miss Weld. Louisa had a few doubts about this arrangement. A traveling companion to an invalid would have to be at that person's beck and call all the time. She wasn't sure she would have the patience. "Go," said both friends and family. So she went.

After an uncomfortable sea journey, she found herself in London. "I feel as if I'd got into a novel. . . ," she wrote, "and thought English weather abominable."

From England they went on to Belgium, Germany, and Switzerland. Castles and cathedrals, the Rhine and Goethe's house, the Alps—Louisa was enchanted by them all. Unfortunately, Miss Weld was more interested in "taking the waters" and sitting in her room than in looking at beautiful things. Louisa didn't feel she could leave the girl alone too often and so missed many sights herself.

Then they came to Vevey, Switzerland, where Miss Weld wanted to rest for a while. They stayed at the Pension Victoria. Here Louisa met a young Polish man, Ladislas Wisinewski. He was "much younger" (twelve or thirteen years) than Louisa, who was thirty-three at the time. Age didn't matter. The two of them became friends at once.

Ladislas taught Louisa French and played the piano for her. She taught him English and made him take care of his cough. Together they went for long walks, sailed on the lake, and talked. Ladislas had been in a nationalist uprising in Poland and had many adventures to tell. In return, Louisa told him about her nursing experiences at Georgetown.

Did they fall in love? Louisa never says. She merely calls him "interesting and good" and mentions that on her birthday, "though nothing very pleasant happened, I was happy and hopeful and enjoyed everything with unusual relish." In her journal, she called Ladislas "Laurie" and later admitted that he was the model for Laurie in *Little Women*.

Miss Weld decided to go on to Nice, where she could soak up the sunshine of the Riviera. Louisa and her Laurie said good-bye and hoped to meet again later in Paris.

Nice, said Louisa, was "very pleasant." Even in sun-drenched Nice, Miss Weld still preferred to spend her days indoors, which was hard on a fresh-air-loving Alcott. In February Louisa told Miss Weld that she would be leaving in May. Miss Weld didn't like this news, but for once Louisa decided to think of herself. "I'm tired of it," she wrote, "and as she is not going to travel, my time is too valuable to be wasted."

On May 1 Louisa set out alone for Paris, "feeling as happy as a freed bird." Laurie was there to meet her and they had two "very charming" weeks together before Louisa went on to England. Somehow Abba Alcott had raised enough money to allow her daughter to complete her travels. From the middle of May until July 7, Louisa roamed around England. This time London was marvelous. She looked at everything, met Gladstone, heard John Stuart Mill speak in Parliament, and listened to Charles Dickens read. And she loved the English countryside even better, "the old farm-house with the thatched roof, the common of yellow gorse, larks going up in the morning, nightingales flying at night, hawthorne everywhere, and Richmond Park full of deer close by."

On July 7 Louisa sailed for home and, after fourteen "stormy, dull, long, sick days" at sea, found "dear John" Pratt waiting to welcome her at the wharf. The next day she went on to Concord and there was "Marmee crying at the door. Into her arms I went, and was home at last.

"Soon fell to work on some stories," she wrote in August, "for things were, as I expected, behindhand when the money-maker was away." Her mother had borrowed the money to keep her in Europe and that, plus other debts, made her pen fly. She wrote for the rest of 1866 and on into 1867.

In September of 1867 Louisa made these notes in her journal: "Niles, partner of Roberts, asked me to write a girls' book. Said I'd try.

"F. asked me to be the editor of 'Merry's Museum.' [a magazine for children] Said I'd try.

"Began at once on both new jobs; but didn't like either."

Little did she know that one of those new jobs was going to change her life and make her dearest dream come true.

In October Louisa packed up her goods once more and rode off to Boston in a wagon, much as Polly traveled to the city in *An Old-Fashioned Girl*. Here she set up housekeeping in a room at No. 6 Hayward Place. She would have more time and peace for her work in Boston, she hoped. And maybe she'd feel better physically too.

She did do a lot of writing, but not on that girls' book. The snow fell and then melted. Her hyacinths bloomed and her pet fly, Buzzy, left the ivy for the flowerpot. Meanwhile, Louisa turned out stories.

February found her back home in Concord again, since her mother wasn't well and needed her. March and April passed. Then, in May, Bronson went to see Mr. Niles of Roberts Brothers about the possibility of Louisa's doing a book of fairy tales for him.

"Mr. N. wants a *girls' story*," wrote Louisa in her journal, "and I begin 'Little Women.' Marmee, Anna, and May all approve my plan. So I plod away, though I don't enjoy this sort of thing. Never liked girls or knew many, except my sisters; but our queer plays and experiences may prove interesting, though I doubt it." ("Good joke," she wrote next to this entry years later.)

In June she sent twelve chapters of "L. W." to Mr. Niles.

He thought they were dull and so did she. She went on with the book anyway, at the same time writing "two tales for Ford, and one for F."

On July 15 she wrote: "Have finished 'Little Women,' and sent it off,—402 pages [written by hand]. . . . Very tired, head full of pain from overwork, and heart heavy about Marmee, who is growing feeble."

In August, "Roberts Bros. made an offer for the story, but at the same time advised me to keep the copyright; so I shall." Keeping the copyright meant that Louisa would have control over what happened to her book in the future. It also meant that she would earn a certain amount of money from each copy that was sold. Otherwise, she would be paid only one lump sum and then no more.

In 1885 she added a note to this journal entry: "An honest publisher and a lucky author, for the copyright made her fortune, and the 'dull book' was the first golden egg of the ugly duckling." Lucky publisher, too, because Louisa went on writing books for him and earned him a fortune as well.

On August 26, the proofs for the book came. "It reads better than I expected," wrote Louisa. "Not a bit sensational, but simple and true, for we really lived most of it, and if it succeeds that will be the reason of it. Mr. N. likes it better now, and says some girls who have read the manuscripts say it is 'splendid!' As it is for them, they are the best critics, so I should be satisfied."

Those girls who first read *Little Women* turned out to be excellent critics, as everyone now knows. By the end of October, one edition had sold out and London wanted a British edition. Mr. Niles was sure he would sell three or four thousand before the end of the year. And he wanted a second volume for spring. (That first book was only what is Part One of today's editions of *Little Women*.)

On November 1, Louisa began Part Two. "A little success is so inspiring that I now find my 'Marches' sober, nice people, and as I can launch into the future, my fancy has more play. Girls write to ask who the little women marry, as if that was the only end and aim of a woman's life. I *won't* marry Jo to Laurie to please any one."

It wasn't that Louisa didn't care about the feelings of her young readers. She simply felt that she knew her characters better than they and that, in Marmee's words, Jo and Laurie just weren't "suited to one another."

Louisa couldn't help but know her characters well. They were the people she had lived with all her life. Later she listed the "facts in the stories that are true, though often changed as to time and place: . . The early plays and experiences; Beth's death; Jo's literary and Amy's artistic experiences; Meg's happy home; John Brooke and his death; Demi's character. Mr. March is all true, only not half good enough. Laurie is not an American boy, though every lad I ever knew claims the character. He was a Polish boy, met abroad in 1865. Mr. Lawrence is my grandfather, Colonel Joseph May. Aunt March is no one."

Louisa loved to play with words, which is how she arrived at some of the names in her books. "March" certainly has something in common with "May," an old family name. And if you switch the letters of "May" around just a bit, you end up with—Amy. Mr. Niles shows up in *Jo's Boys* as Mr. Tiber (both names of rivers). There are other little jokes too, waiting for readers who look for them.

On January 1, 1869, Louisa sent Part Two off to Mr. Niles, no doubt with a great sigh of relief. Her relief was even greater, though, when in March she was able to write: "Paid up all the debts, thank the Lord!—every penny that money can pay,—and now feel as if I could die in peace. My dream is beginning to come true; and if my head holds out I'll do all I once hoped to do."

Chapter 10

THE GOLDEN EGGS

> *Long ago in a poultry yard*
> *One dull November morn,*
> *Beneath a motherly soft wing*
> *A little goose was born.*

> . . . .

> *She could not sing, she could not fly,*
> *Nor even walk with grace,*
> *And all the farm-yard had declared*
> *A puddle was her place.*

> . . . .

> *At length she came unto a stream*
> *Most fertile of all* Niles,
> *Where tuneful birds might soar and sing*
> *Among the leafy isles.*

> . . . .

> *And here she paused to smooth her plumes,*
> *Ruffled by many plagues;*
> *When suddenly arose the cry,*
> *"This goose lays golden eggs."*

From THE LAY OF THE GOLDEN GOOSE
by Louisa May Alcott

Little Women certainly was a golden egg, although even Louisa did not yet realize how golden it would prove to be. What she did realize was what a fine publisher she had found in Roberts Brothers. She told Mr. Niles so. "After toiling so many years along the uphill road,—always a hard one to women writers,—" she wrote, "it is peculiarly grateful to me to find the way growing easier at last, with pleasant little surprises blossoming on either side, and the rough places made smooth by the courtesy and kindness of those who have proved themselves friends as well as publishers."

Sharing responsibility with someone must have been a delightful new experience for Louisa. She wrote good books and sent them to Mr. Niles. He did a good job of publishing and selling them and sent her money. It was a partnership, and Louisa hadn't known many of those since she had grown up. Mostly she had had to do everything on her own.

Louisa obviously loved her family and they loved her. But families sometimes get used to leaning on one strong person and forget that that person has needs too. A sad little journal entry on Louisa's thirty-sixth birthday seems to show that this was true for her: "My birthday; thirty-six. Spent alone, writing hard. No presents but Father's 'Tablets' [a book Bronson had written].

"I never seem to have many presents, as some do, though I give a good many. That is best perhaps, and makes a gift very precious when it does come."

Surely Anna, happily settled now, could have sent her something. Or May, to whom she gave so much.

Louisa's family did not seem worried about her health either, although she often mentioned pains in her legs and head, dizziness, and an inability to sleep. Part of the problem might have been that no one knew what was bothering her. Her family might have thought that she was simply being a "typical spinster," fussing too much about her little aches and pains. They could not have known what medical authorities later suspected to have been the cause of her prolonged illness.

When Louisa was sick with typhoid pneumonia, she had been given huge doses of calomel. This was the best cure doctors knew then—and it worked. But calomel contains great quantities of mercury, which remains in the body and slowly poisons it. When she was in Europe, Louisa met a man who suffered from the same symptoms after taking calomel for a jungle fever. He believed that iodine of potash would cure the condition. Louisa took it faithfully, but it didn't help her much.

Sometimes Louisa suffered a great deal; sometimes she seemed to feel better. No matter how she felt, she went on working. In the fall of 1869, she and May shared rooms in Pinckney Street in Boston, and Louisa began *An Old-Fashioned Girl*. She finished it in February and noted: "I wrote it with left hand in a sling, one foot up, head aching, and no voice. Yet, as the book is funny, people will say,

'Didn't you enjoy it?' . . . I certainly earn my living by the sweat of my brow."

However bad she felt, she must have thoroughly enjoyed writing her opening to the last chapter, where she says: " . . . Intimidated by the threats, denunciations, and complaints showered upon me in consequence of taking the liberty to end a certain story as I liked, I now yield to the amiable desire of giving satisfaction, and, at the risk of outraging all the unities, intend to pair off everybody I can lay my hands on." Her readers must have given her a lot of trouble, indeed, for not marrying Jo to Laurie!

With *Little Women* doing well and a new edition of *Hospital Sketches*, plus *An Old-Fashioned Girl*, now published, Louisa decided that she could give herself a well-deserved vacation. On April 2, 1870, she, May, and Alice Bartlett, a friend of May's, set off to travel around Europe.

This was a very different sort of trip from Louisa's first one, although she was seasick again. Once the boat docked, the three women began to enjoy themselves with all their might. They wandered from sight to sight, staring, sketching, and stumbling along in their dreadful French. They rode in carts pulled by donkeys, were attacked by pigs, explored ruined castles, and ate so much that they got "fat and hearty."

Sometimes Louisa received letters from various editors, asking for more stories. "I am truly grateful," she wrote to

Mr. Niles, "but having come abroad for rest I am not inclined to try the treadmill till my year's vacation is over. So to appease these worthy gentlemen and excuse my seeming idleness I send you a trifle in rhyme ["The Lay of the Golden Goose"], which you can (if you think it worth the trouble) set going as a general answer to everybody; . . ."

Not even the outbreak of a "silly little war" between France and Prussia could curb the spirits of the three travelers, although it did force them to hurry off to Italy sooner than they had planned. There, in Rome, they received sad news from home. John Pratt had died, leaving Anna a widow with two sons to raise.

Louisa didn't know what to do. She wanted to rush home. On the other hand, May was getting so much out of her art studies in Italy that it seemed a shame to stop them. Louisa decided that the answer was for her to write another book, a sequel to *Little Women*, to be called *Little Men*. All the proceeds from the new book would go to Anna and the children. Without a single squawk of protest, the golden goose took three more charges under her protective wing.

By May Louisa was ready to go home, even though her sister chose to stay longer. This time Bronson and Mr. Niles met her. On their carriage was a bright poster that said: LITTLE MEN. The book had come out that very day and had already sold fifty thousand copies!

Back in Concord, Bronson had another surprise for her.

He had earned some money giving talks and had redecorated her bedroom. Louisa was not only surprised, but deeply touched. Even so, in October she moved to Boston again. By November, though, she could see that her family needed someone to take charge. Anna and her boys were living at Orchard House, but Anna was still too lost in her grief to be much help. And Abba Alcott was not at all well.

For once Louisa did not hurry home herself. Instead, she wrote to May in Europe and told her that she was needed. May packed up, at once came home, and took over. She had only needed to be asked.

With her worry over her family relieved, Louisa wrote away until spring—an account of her travels through France, called *Shawl-Straps*, and a sketch called "A French Wedding." In the spring she went home to help May and then returned to Boston the following autumn.

That same year (1872), she finished a book for adults that she had begun long ago. Called *Work*, it told the story of a girl trying to make her own way in the world. *Work* came out both as a serial and in book form in the United States and England. Unfortunately, it never became a great success.

Meanwhile, Louisa traveled back and forth—warm months in Concord and cold ones in Boston. Her health continued to give her problems, and she was desperately worried about Abba, who had grown very feeble. At least money was no longer a problem. She could easily afford to send May back to Europe and could buy her mother all the comforts she needed. She even had money left over to invest. That must have made her pen feel lighter as she sat down in 1874 to write *Eight Cousins*.

Louisa's success as an author was doing Bronson some good too. He gave a series of lectures in the West in 1875. Bronson said he was "riding in Louisa's chariot, and adored as the grandfather of 'Little Women.' "

As far as Louisa was concerned, she could do without fame. "This is my worst scrape," she confessed to her journal in the summer of 1875. "I asked for bread, and got a stone,—in the shape of a pedestal." Collecting autographs and souvenirs of famous people was as much the rage back then as it is now. Ninety-two guests showed up at Orchard House in one month that summer. No doubt some of them were welcome. But some must have been like the visitors Louisa later described in "Jo's Last Scrape," a chapter in *Jo's Boys*.

We know that the lady from Oshkosh descended on Louisa much as she descended on Jo, although Louisa actually met her at a congress on women's rights that she attended that fall. "If you ever come to Oshkosh," gushed this lady, as she pumped away at Louisa's arm, "your feet will not be allowed to touch the ground: you will be borne in the arms of the people! Will you come?"

"Never," replied Louisa, trying not to laugh.

In November she paid a visit to New York. There she

made many new friends, who treated the " 'umble Concord worm" graciously. She also spent some time with poor children at the newsboys' home, orphanages, hospitals, and insane asylums. Such places were crowded in those days with "poor babies, born of want and sin, suffering every sort of deformity, disease, and pain." Louisa celebrated Christmas by handing out at least two hundred dolls.

Her sorrow for such children ran deep and came out strongly in such characters as Jane in *An Old-Fashioned Girl* and Nat, Dan, Dick, and Billy in *Little Men*. She also believed that more fortunate people had a responsibility to the poor and helpless—and could receive a great deal from them in return. Both Polly and Miss Mills speak this belief in *An Old-Fashioned Girl*.

The year 1876 brought a sequel to *Eight Cousins—Rose in Bloom*. (Rose was another character who received more than she gave by helping poor people.) Louisa wrote the book while nursing her mother in Concord. That year she also helped Anna buy a home nearby for herself and the boys.

May was back in Europe again and doing well with her art. "The money I invested in her pays the sort of interest I like," wrote Louisa. "I am proud to have her show what she can do, and have her depend upon no one but me. Success to little Raphael! My dull winter is much cheered by her happiness and success."

Louisa managed to cheer up the rest of that "dull winter"

herself by writing a very different kind of book. Roberts Brothers had a "No Name Series" for which famous authors wrote without putting their names on their books. It was up to the public to decide who wrote what.

The idea sounded like a fine joke to Louisa, so she contributed an adult book called *A Modern Mephistopheles*. It was a tragic tale about a young poet and owed a lot to her old hero, Goethe. Louisa couldn't help but chuckle when the book came out and several critics declared that it must have been written by Nathaniel Hawthorne's son, Julian.

During the summer of 1877, both she and her mother were sick. Nevertheless, Louisa began work on another children's book, *Under the Lilacs*. She finished it as she sat beside Abba's bed. Abba was dying now, as both she and Louisa knew. "Stay by, Louy," she said, "and help me if I suffer too much."

Louisa stayed, even though she became so ill herself that for a while the family thought she might die first. Fortunately she didn't, and both women were moved to Anna's house where they could receive better care. Abba remained there about a week. Then, one rainy Sunday evening in November, she died peacefully in Louisa's arms.

Abba Alcott was buried in Sleepy Hollow cemetery beside Elizabeth. "I never wish her back," wrote Louisa in December, "but a great warmth seems gone out of life, and there is no motive to go on now.

"My only comfort is that I *could* make her last years comfortable, and lift off the burden she had carried so bravely all these years."

In February Louisa wrote a poem about her mother, calling it "Transfigurations." The last two stanzas are:

> *Oh, noble woman! never more a queen*
> *Than in laying down*
> *Of sceptre and of crown*
> *To win a greater kingdom, yet unseen:*

> *Teaching us how to seek the highest goal,*
> *To earn the true success,—*
> *To live, to love, to bless,—*
> *And make death proud to take a royal soul.*

Chapter 11

THE PATIENT HEART

I am no longer eager, bold, and strong,—
All that is past;
I am ready not to do
At last—at last.
My half-day's work is done,
And this is all my part.
I give a patient God
My patient heart.

Found by Louisa under a soldier's
pillow in the hospital

May did not come home from Europe for her mother's last illness and death. "It was best not to send for her," wrote Louisa, "and Marmee forbade it, and she has some very *tender friends* near her." It was left to Anna to care for Louisa now, who was suffering physically as well as from grief.

In March of 1878, May sent news that cheered everyone. She had married a "tender friend," Ernest Nieriker, a Swiss businessman. Louisa was very happy for May and sent a thousand dollars for a wedding gift.

The life of the newlyweds sounded a lot like that of Amy and Laurie in *Little Women*. Ernest, a violinist himself, was proud of his wife's artistic talent and sometimes posed for her or read to her as she painted. In the evenings they both relaxed with music. Louisa must have been pleased at how her prophecy had come true, even though the groom wasn't *her* Laurie. (May had met Ladislas in Paris, but their friendship never grew and eventually faded.)

Both May and Ernest wanted Louisa to visit them at their home in Meudon. Louisa even made plans to sail in September. Then, at the last minute, she changed her mind. What if she became ill in France, she worried. She couldn't bear to be a burden on the young people. Then Anna broke her leg, and Louisa settled down to nurse her.

They were now all making their home in the house Louisa had helped Anna buy. Louisa wrote that they would never go back to Orchard House. "It ceased to be 'home' when Marmee left it." She and her father carried red leaves and flowers to the Sleepy Hollow cemetery on Abba's birthday, October 8. "A cold, dull day," Louisa wrote, "and I was glad there was no winter for her any more."

The next year, 1879, brought more happy news from May. She and Ernest were expecting a child in the autumn. All the Alcotts rejoiced, and Louisa fixed up "a box of dainty things" to send the expectant mother.

In June Louisa went with Bronson to visit a men's prison.

There she told the prisoners a "hospital story with a little moral to it," which some of them seemed to like very much. A year and a half later, one of those prisoners, now free, came to tell her how much the story had meant to him. It had convinced him that it was never too late to begin again, and that was just what he meant to do with a new job in South America. This incident, changed a good bit, found its way into Dan's adventures in *Jo's Boys*.

At this time Louisa was writing mostly short tales for children. She didn't feel well enough to take on a longer book just yet. She probably didn't have the time either, as great things were happening at Orchard House. A School of Philosophy was opening, with Bronson Alcott as dean. Thirty philosophers came from all over to meet and study there that first summer. Bronson was, as Louisa put it, "in his glory." Of course she had helped this dream come true, even though she had less and less patience with philosophers. "If they were philanthropists, I should enjoy it," she wrote, "but speculation seems a waste of time when there is so much real work crying to be done. Why discuss the 'unknowable' till our poor are fed and the wicked saved?"

Louisa had a glorious moment herself when she "was the first woman to register my name as a voter [in Concord]." She tried to get other women interested in suffrage too, but found it "so hard to move people out of the old ruts."

By September she was at work on another book, *Jack and*

Jill, which would appear first as a serial in *St. Nicholas* magazine. Her heroes and heroines were to be children from Concord, who followed the progress of the book with tremendous excitement.

On November 8, Louisa wrote in her journal: "Little Louisa May Nieriker arrived in Paris at 9 P.M., after a short journey. All doing well. Much rejoicing. Nice little lass, and May very happy. Ah, if I had only been there!"

Then, at the beginning of December: "May not doing well. The weight on my heart is not all imagination. She was too happy to have it last. . . ."

On December 31, Anna was away in Boston and Bronson was at the post office, checking for letters from France. Louisa came in to find Mr. Emerson holding a paper in his hand and looking at May's portrait with tears in his eyes. "My child, I wish I could prepare you; but alas, alas!" he said and handed Louisa a telegram.

"I *am* prepared," she said and read the "hard words" that told her May was dead. Ernest had sent the telegram to Mr. Emerson so he could break the news. Later, letters explained that it had been a peaceful death and that May had had time to arrange things as she wished them. She wanted Louisa to have her baby and her pictures. Little Lulu was to come in the spring (later postponed till autumn).

"Shall I ever know why such things happen?" Louisa grieved in her journal.

"I cannot make it true that our May is dead, lying far away in a strange grave. . . ."

Nothing she did seemed to help the pain in her heart. "Tried to write on 'J. and J.' to distract my mind," she wrote in January of 1880, "but the wave of sorrow kept rolling over me, and I could only weep and wait till the tide ebbed again."

Somehow, though, she did finish *Jack and Jill.* "Both these last serials were written with a heavy heart—" she told her journal, " 'Under the Lilacs' when Marmee was failing, and 'Jack and Jill' while May was dying. Hope the grief did not get into them."

Life went on, and Louisa always managed to count her blessings. "Got gifts for Anna's birthday on the 16th,—forty-nine years old," she wrote in March. "My only sister now, and the best God ever made." She didn't do much writing for a while, but she did keep busy with her work for the poor and for women's rights. And she prepared for Lulu.

This *"very* remarkable child" arrived on September 18. Louisa had sent a Mrs. Giles to travel back with the baby and May's sister-in-law, Sophie Nieriker. But it was the ship's captain, himself, who handed the baby to Louisa. "I held out my arms to Lulu, only being able to say her name," she later wrote in her journal. "She looked at me for a moment, then came to me, saying 'Marmar' in a wistful way, and resting close as if she had found her own people and home at last, . . ."

The next years were busy ones for Louisa, not so much with her writing as with "my baby." On December 23, 1880, "she got up and walked alone. . . ." By February 21, 1881, Lulu showed that she had inherited her mother's artistic taste. She preferred the pictures of two great children's artists, Caldecott and Greenaway.

In December of 1881, Louisa noted: "A poor woman in Illinois writes me to send her children some Christmas gifts, being too poor and ill to get any. They asked her to write to Santa Claus and she wrote to *me*. Sent a box . . . . Lulu much interested, and kept bringing all her best toys and clothes 'for poor little boys.' A generous baby."

April of 1882 brought Louisa another sorrow, the death of Mr. Emerson. "Our best and greatest American gone," she wrote. "The nearest and dearest friend Father has ever had, and the man who has helped me most by his life, his books, his society. I can never tell all he has been to me. . . ."

In October Louisa left Lulu with Anna for a short while and went to Boston to begin work on *Jo's Boys*, the last of the books about the March family. Later that month, on October 24, she received a telegram telling her that Bronson had had a paralytic stroke. From then on, Louisa juggled three full-time jobs—caring for him, bringing up Lulu, and writing.

Sometimes she lived in Concord, sometimes in Boston. In June of 1884 she bought a cottage by the sea, where she and Anna could take turns having a month of vacation. Her own illness was giving her a lot of trouble again and she could write only for short periods of time. Still she plugged away at *Jo's Boys*.

The book was finally published in 1886. Louisa's preface gives a hint of what she must have gone through to finish it: "Having been written at long intervals during the past seven years, this story is more faulty than any of its very imperfect predecessors; but the desire to atone for an unavoidable disappointment, and to please my patient little friends, has urged me to let it go without further delay.

"To account for the seeming neglect of Amy, let me add, that, since the original of that character died, it has been impossible for me to write of her as when she was here to suggest, criticise, and laugh over her namesake. The same applies to Marmee. But the folded leaves are not blank to those who knew and loved them and can find memorials of them in whatever is cheerful, true, or helpful in these pages."

Jo's Boys was the last novel Louisa wrote. She did, however, have ideas for collections of short stories for children. For older girls there was *A Garland for Girls*. For little children there was *Lulu's Library*, three books of stories that she had originally written for Lulu herself. Some of her earlier stories had also been collected into books—*Silver Pitchers, Proverb Stories, Spinning-Wheel Stories, My Boys, Shawl-Straps, Cupid and Chow-Chow, My Girls, Jimmy's Cruise in the Pinafore,* and *An Old-Fashioned Thanksgiving.*

Otherwise, Louisa's health prevented her from doing much work. She did have a fine doctor now, Rhoda Lawrence, who soon became her close friend too. Dr. Lawrence urged rest, along with her other remedies, and Louisa was glad to follow that prescription. Eventually she moved into the doctor's house in Roxbury, leaving only for short visits to her family.

On October 16, 1887, Louisa sent her aunt, Mrs. Bond, a letter with the little poem that she had found under a soldier's pillow. In that same letter, she says: "The learning not to do is so hard after being the hub to the family wheel so long. But it is good for the energetic ones to find that the world can get on without them, and to learn to be still, to give up, and wait cheerfully."

The last thing she wrote was another letter to that aunt. She closed it: "Slow climbing, but I don't slip back, so think up my mercies, and sing cheerfully, as dear Marmee used to do, 'Thus far the Lord has led me on!' "

Louisa had prepared for death. She had read and destroyed her mother's journal. She had burned any of her own letters that she felt should have been kept private. She had officially adopted her younger nephew, John, so that he could be her legal heir and carry on the Alcott name. Lulu, she knew, would be well cared for by the child's father's family in Europe.

One day, early in March, Louisa went to see her father,

who had grown very weak. She suspected that this would be the last time she would see him and was, of course, troubled by the possibility. When she left her father, Louisa forgot to put on her warm cloak. The next day she had an agonizing headache and, by afternoon, was unconscious. At 3:30 P.M. on March 6, 1888, Louisa May Alcott died. She did not know that her father had slipped into death just before her.

Louisa had written a poem for Bronson on his eighty-sixth birthday. With just a few changes, the last stanza of that poem might be for her, as well:

> The staff set by, the sandals off,
>   Still pondering the precious scroll,
> Serene and strong, she waits the call
>   That frees and wings a happy soul.
> Then, beautiful as when it lured
>   The girl's aspiring eyes,
> Before the pilgrim's longing sight
>   Shall the Celestial City rise.

Louisa's body was buried at Sleepy Hollow cemetery, lying crossways at feet of her mother, father, and sister.

Works by Louisa May Alcott

For Children

(Novels) *Little Women* (1868-69), *An Old-Fashioned Girl* (1870), *Little Men* (1871), *Eight Cousins* (1875), *Rose in Bloom* (1876), *Under the Lilacs* (1878), *Jack and Jill* (1880), *Jo's Boys* (1886), *A Garland for Girls* (1888)

(Collections) *Flower Fables* (1854); *Aunt Jo's Scrapbag* (6 volumes, 1872-82); *My Boys* (1872); *Shawl-Straps* (1872); *Cupid and Chow-Chow* (1874); *My Girls* (1878); *Jimmy's Cruise in the Pinafore* (1879); *An Old-Fashioned Thanksgiving* (1882); *Silver Pitchers* (1876); *Proverb Stories* (1882); *Spinning-Wheel Stories* (1884); *Lulu's Library* (3 volumes, 1886-89), Volume I (1886), Volume II (1887), Volume III (1889)

For Adults

Hospital Sketches (1863), *Moods* (1864), *Work* (1873), *A Modern Mephistopheles* (1877)

Louisa May Alcott's Advice to a Young Writer

Dear Sir,—I never copy or "polish," so I have no old manuscripts to send you; and if I had it would be of little use, for one person's method is no rule for another. Each must work in his own way; and the only drill needed is to keep writing and profit by criticism. Mind grammar, spelling, and punctuation, use short words, and express as briefly as you can your meaning. Young people use too many adjectives and try to "write fine." The strongest, simplest words are best, and no *foreign* ones if it can be helped.

Write, and print if you can; if not, still write, and improve as you go on. Read the best books, and they will improve your style. See and hear good speakers and wise people, and learn of them. Work for twenty years, and then you may some day find that you have a style and place of your own, and can command good pay for the same things no one would take when you were unknown.

I know little of poetry, as I never read modern attempts, but advise any young person to keep to prose, as only once in a century is there a true poet; and verses are so easy to do that it is not much help to write them. I have so many letters like your own that I can say no more, but wish you success, and give you for a motto Michael Angelo's wise words: "Genius is infinite patience."

Your friend, L. M. Alcott

P. S.—The lines you send are much better than many I see; but boys of nineteen cannot know much about hearts, and had better write of things they understand. Sentiment is apt to become sentimentality; and sense is always safer, as well as better drill, for young fancies and feelings.

Read Ralph Waldo Emerson, and see what good prose is, and some of the best poetry we have. I much prefer him to Longfellow.

(Letter to Mr. J. P. True, dated October 24, no year given)

Louisa May Alcott 1832-1888

1832 Black Hawk War in Illinois, Indians defeated. Italy is founded; its goal is the unification of Italy. First railroad in Europe is completed. Louisa May Alcott is born in Germantown, Pennsylvania.

1833 An early version of baseball is played for the first time in the United States. Slavery abolished in British Empire.

1834 Whig Party is founded in United States. Cyrus H. McCormick patents his reaper. Americans first to eat tomatoes.

1835 Unsuccessful attempt to assassinate President Jackson. Halley's Comet seen. Hans Christian Anderson, a Dane, first publishes fairy tales.

1836 Texas becomes independent. *McGuffey's Reader* becomes standard textbook in United States. Dickens publishes *Pickwick Papers.*

1837 Economic depression begins in the United States. First kindergarten opened in Germany. Victoria becomes queen in England. Dickens publishes *Oliver Twist.*

1838 Cherokee Nation moved to eastern Oklahoma. Start of Underground Railroad in the United States. Famine in north of Ireland.

1839 First form of photography invented by Louis Daguerre, a Frenchman.

1841 President Harrison dies one month after inauguration. James Fenimore Cooper publishes *The Deerslayer.*

1844 Samuel Morse sends first telegraph message, "What hath God wrought!"

1845 Texas is annexed to the United States. Edgar Allan Poe publishes *The Raven.* Irish potato famine.

1846 Beginning of United States war with Mexico.

1848 Treaty of Guadalupe Hidalgo ends Mexican War. Karl Marx, a German, issues *Communist Manifesto.*

1851 Nathaniel Hawthorne publishes *The House of the Seven Gables.*

1852 Harriet Beecher Stowe publishes *Uncle Tom's Cabin.*

1854 Kansas-Nebraska Act repeals 1820 Missouri Compromise; Republican Party established as reaction against act. Louisa May Alcott publishes her first book, *Flower Fables.*

1856 Abolitionist John Brown and his forces murder pro-slavery settlers at Pottawatomie Creek in Kansas.

1857 Dred Scott Decision by U.S. Supreme Court—Negro slave is found to be still a slave even if living in free territory. Also, Missouri Compromise declared unconstitutional.

1858 Lincoln-Douglas debates during Illinois Senate race; issue is slavery.

1859 Abolitionist John Brown is hanged after he tries to start a slave revolt. Darwin publishes *Origin of Species.* First successful oil well drilled at Titusville, Pennsylvania. Dickens publishes *A Tale of Two Cities.*

1860 Abraham Lincoln is elected president; South Carolina secedes from the Union.

1861 Civil War begins. Prince Albert, Queen Victoria's husband, dies. Tzar Alexander II frees Russian serfs. Kingdom of Italy is born; Victor Emmanuel II is king. *Silas Marner* by George Eliot is published in England.

1862 Civil War battles of Shiloh, Second Battle of Bull Run, Antietam, Fredericksburg are fought, among others. Louisa May Alcott becomes nurse for Union side.

1863 Lincoln issues Emancipation Proclamation freeing slaves in Confederate states.

Confederate forces defeated at the Battle of Gettysburg.

1864 General Sherman's march to the sea; Atlanta is burned. Lincoln reelected. Louisa May Alcott publishes *Moods*.

1865 Civil War ends; Lincoln assassinated. Lewis Carroll, English novelist, publishes *Alice's Adventures in Wonderland*.

1866 Congress passes the 14th Amendment which guarantees civil rights for freed Negroes.

1867 Three Reconstruction Acts passed; U.S. buys Alaska from Russia. A Swede, Alfred Nobel, patents dynamite. Marx publishes volume I of *Das Kapital*. In Mexico, Emperor Maximilian is executed. Military rule is abolished in Japan.

1868 President Johnson impeached by House, acquitted by Senate. U.S. Grant elected president. Revolution in Spain; Queen Isabella II deposed. Meiji dynasty restored in Japan.

1869 The world's first transcontinental railroad is finished; east and west sections meet in Promontory, Utah. Louisa May Alcott publishes *Little Women*. Suez Canal opens.

1870 Louisa May Alcott finishes *An Old-Fashioned Girl*. Beginning of Franco-Prussian War. Revolution in France.

1871 Treaty of Frankfurt ends Franco-Prussian War. William Marcy (Boss) Tweed indicted for fraud in New York City. Feudalism banned in Japan. Louisa May Alcott publishes *Little Men*.

1872 Lewis Carroll publishes *Through the Looking Glass*. Louisa May Alcott finishes an adult book, *Work*.

1874 Disraeli becomes British prime minister, second time. National Woman's Christian Temperance Union is formed in Cleveland. Louisa May Alcott writes *Eight Cousins*.

1876 Battle of Little Bighorn; General Custer defeated by Sioux and Cheyenne. Alexander Graham Bell patents telephone. Mark Twain publishes *The Adventures of Tom Sawyer*. Louisa May Alcott writes *Rose in Bloom*.

1877 Reconstruction ends in the South. Porfirio Diaz becomes president of Mexico. Rebellion put down in Japan.

1878 In the United States, Albert A. Michelson accurately measures speed of light at 186,508 miles per second. Edison patents the phonograph.

1879 Edison invents first practical electric light. Afghans cede Khyber Pass, among other territories, to the British.

1880 Joel Chandler Harris publishes *Uncle Remus: His Songs and Sayings*.

1881 President Garfield is assassinated in Washington, D.C. Mark Twain publishes *The Prince and the Pauper*. Alexander II of Russia is assassinated.

1882 Ralph Waldo Emerson dies.

1883 Discovery by Edison that electric current can be sent through space. Twain publishes *Life on the Mississippi*. Scottish writer Robert Lewis Stevenson publishes *Treasure Island*. Program of social reform begun in Germany.

1884 Ottmar Mergenthaler, a German-American, patents the Linotype machine, a typesetting machine that casts one line at a time. Twain publishes *The Adventures of Huckleberry Finn*.

1885 Frenchman Louis Pasteur develops rabies vaccination.

1886 Louisa May Alcott publishes *Jo's Boys*. The Statue of Liberty is dedicated in New York harbor. War with Apaches ends with Chief Geronimo's surrender.

1887 U.S. obtains right to build naval base at Pearl Harbor in Hawaii. Queen Victoria of England celebrates Golden Jubilee. French form Indo-China.

1888 Louisa May Alcott dies in Roxbury, Massachusetts.

INDEX- *Page numbers in boldface type indicate illustrations.*

125

ABOUT THE AUTHOR

Carol Greene has a B.A. in English Literature from Park College, Parkville, Missouri and an M.A. in Musicology from Indiana University, Bloomington. She's worked with international exchange programs, taught music and writing, and edited children's books. Ms. Greene now works as a free-lance writer in St. Louis, Missouri and has published over forty books. Some of her other books for Childrens Press include *The Thirteen Days of Halloween, A Computer Went A-Courting*, four in the *Enchantment of the World* series—*England, Poland, Japan*, and *Yugoslavia*—and *Marie Curie: Pioneer Physicist* in this series.